FIRST MATE

Susan Macias

A KISMET™ Romance

METEOR PUBLISHING CORPORATION
Bensalem, Pennsylvania

SUSAN MACIAS

Susan Macias has always read romances. In the eighth grade, she got in trouble for hiding one behind her algebra book in class. She gave up a promising career in accounting to try her hand at writing and has never looked back. Susan lives in Southern California with her husband. The prolific author loves hearing from readers. You may write her directly at: P.O. Box 11022, Canoga Park, CA 91304.

PROLOGUE

Amy hurried across the lawn, smoothing her skirt down as she went. The photographer was taking pictures inside the smaller of the striped tents. Her mother—the bride—had sent her off to fix her hair. If she didn't rush back, they would take the photos without her.

If only Nappy were here, she thought as she made her way through the crowd of wedding guests. He'd make sure she didn't get left out. But the old man was spending the spring in Greece. Knowing he was now officially her step-grandfather, only made the pain of missing him worse.

Rounding the corner, she came to an abrupt halt. The entire wedding party stood arranged in a perfect half circle, her stunning mother and sisters next to each other. There was no room for her. She'd been forgotten again.

Amy bit down hard on her lip, then started backing

up. If someone in the tent saw her, they'd just pretend they'd been waiting for her all along. Her mother would smile coldly and kiss the air next to her cheek. Not today, she thought as she turned and ran. She couldn't play the game anymore.

Her flight was halted when she bumped into something solid and warm. Hands gripped her arms, keeping her from tumbling to the ground. Blinking through the tears, she saw the vague outline of a man. Her vision cleared and her heart leapt in her chest. It was him!

In the weeks before the wedding, she'd overheard heated conversations about whether or not *he* should be allowed to attend. Her mother had been resistant, but Amy's soon-to-be stepfather had insisted an invitation be mailed. Despite her mother's hopes that the guest in question would have the good sense to stay away, the prodigal son had decided to return.

Earlier this morning, Amy had watched him drive up to the house. His sleek, black motorcycle had seemed out of place next to the elegant Mercedes her mother owned.

Torn between curiosity and her natural reticence around a good-looking young man, Amy had kept her distance. Even now, with his strong hands holding her steady, she searched her mind for something witty to say. But she'd always been the shy one. Her best friend, Rachel, would have already introduced herself and had him laughing at some well-timed joke. Amy only felt awkward.

"Hi," she managed finally, the single word sticking in her throat like a crumb of dried bread.

"Hi, yourself. I was hoping we'd get a chance to

meet before I had to take off. Nappy's told me a lot about you.''

"Really?'' She silently groaned at the childish pleasure in her voice. Couldn't she, for once, sound sophisticated?

He looked down at her. His face reminded her of a picture of a statue she'd seen once. High cheekbones were sculpted beneath golden skin. A narrow nose cut a clean path to straight, uncompromising lips. The beard hid the lines of his jaw, but he was still incredibly handsome. Rachel was going to die when she told her about him.

He released her, but didn't move back. Amy saw that he'd discarded his morning coat and was once again in jeans and a cotton shirt. Despite the Florida heat, a black leather jacket hung over one arm.

"Where are you off to in such a hurry?'' he asked.

"I . . .'' She brushed the moisture from her cheeks, then looked away. "Nowhere.''

He moved beside her and glanced into the tent. "Photographs, huh? Why aren't you there?''

She shrugged. "I don't like having my picture taken.''

Brown eyes studied her, seeing past the casual lie. "A pretty girl like you?''

She could feel the heat creeping up her face. Not now, she pleaded.

"Come on.'' He pressed his hand against the small of her back and urged her toward the front of the house.

She stumbled slightly, then walked beside him, her legs unable to keep up with his longer stride. "Where are we going?''

"I'm taking you for a ride on my bike.''

"But I . . ." She glanced back at the tent. "Shouldn't you be in there with the wedding party?"

"No." A bitter line replaced the smile on his lips. "I don't like having my picture taken, either."

When they reached the motorcycle, Amy hesitated. "Maybe I should tell someone where I'm going."

"We'll be back before they miss you."

Amy felt tears burning behind her lids, but she blinked them away. He was right. Besides, they'd never miss *her*. "Sure. Let's go."

He set a helmet on her head and adjusted the chin strap to its tightest setting. Even so, the bubble of plastic slid wildly over her hair.

He grinned. "It'll have to do. I'll drive slow." He swung one jean-clad leg across the seat, then looked over his shoulder. "Climb on behind me and hold tight."

Amy copied his motion. The full skirt of her dress hung past her feet and she bunched it between her knees. Even with the barrier of fabric, she could feel the heat of his body as she tentatively placed her hands on his back. Hold on? To a stranger . . . a man? She couldn't.

"No. Like this." He grabbed her hands and pulled them until her arms were firmly wrapped around his waist. After turning the starter, he gunned the motor and put the powerful machine in gear. They moved down the long driveway and out toward the beach.

The sun was high in the sky and the breeze from the blue ocean brushed her face. As they rode along the coast, Amy stared at the world around her. She'd never felt so free before. The dress billowed out behind her like a parachute. She bit back a yelp of excitement and quickly tucked the skirt under her legs.

He leaned into a turn and she followed suit. The slow beat of his heart bumped against her left hand. She was going to die. Right here on the main boulevard in front of God and everybody, she was going to die. This was the most exciting experience of her life. *Don't scream,* she warned herself as she felt the pressure build in her chest.

She leaned forward and muffled the shriek of delight against his back. Inhaling deeply, she smelled leather and something else. A spicy, musky scent that was unfamiliar, but not unpleasant. Her heart skipped about a thousand beats.

"I don't want to go back," she whispered.

But he didn't hear her. He turned at the next corner and drove up the driveway.

"Home, safe and sound." He stepped off, then helped her down from the bike. "How'd you like it?"

"It was . . ." His fingers touched her face as he unbuckled the strap. ". . . wonderful. Thank you, Napoleon."

He winced visibly. "Don't call me that."

"It's your name."

"Napoleon Christopher Spirno isn't a name, it's a curse. I go by Mac."

"Why?"

He grinned. "It's short and everybody can spell it. I gotta go, Amy, but it was nice meeting you."

"What about the reception? They haven't cut the cake yet."

"You can have my slice."

"Will I see you again?" She twisted her hands together, barely daring to meet his eyes. He was older; twenty-three, Nappy had said.

He shrugged and glanced at the house. "I don't know. I don't get back to see my father very often these days."

"My birthday's next month. There'll be a big dinner." She hated the hopeful pleading in her voice, but didn't retract the implied invitation.

"How old will you be?"

"S–sixteen."

His smile was slow and lazy. "Sweet sixteen and never been kissed?"

"I . . ." She stared at the ground. It wasn't *her* fault she went to an all-girl boarding school. A boy had tried, last summer on the beach, but his alcohol-laced breath made her duck away.

But Mac wasn't a boy . . . he was a man. Although he reminded her of Nappy, whom she loved more than anyone in the world, there was an element of danger that made him different from anyone in her cloistered circle. Everything she had heard made him seem larger than life.

"I'm sure the boys will figure out what they've been missing," he said, staring down at her.

"I hope so."

"Trust me. You've got nothing to worry about."

There was an odd light in his eyes, an emotion she couldn't read and didn't understand. One finger tilted her chin until she was forced to stare into chocolate-brown eyes. He lowered his mouth. Amy felt her body stiffen as warm lips pressed against hers. There was a sensation of strength . . . and softness, along with the strange tickling of his mustache and beard. She was close enough to see the individual lashes resting against his cheek. Her arms hung at her sides, her fists buried in the folds of her skirt.

He raised his head. "You pack quite a punch, little Amy. You almost make me wish I could stick around."

He swung one long leg over the motorcycle and turned the key. The powerful engine roared to life. He jerked his head toward the house. "Don't let the bastards get you down, princess."

"I won't," she whispered, touching her fingers to her still tingling lips. But the promise was lost as he turned the machine and rode down the driveway. She'd finally met her stepbrother. How long would it be until she saw him again?

ONE

Beep

Mac glared at the computer screen. The flashing cursor glared back. Neither blinked . . . unless he counted the incessant flashing. *Enter total for accounts receivable*, the program instructed. But he didn't have the total. If he had the total, he wouldn't need the damn computer in the first place.

Leaning back in his chair with a sigh, Mac swiveled toward the huge window behind his desk. The warm Florida day beckoned. Blue sky competed with even bluer ocean. The temperature was balmy, the breeze snapped just enough to promise a perfect sail. Instead of skimming across the water in his thirty-six-foot sloop, he was stuck in the office with a recalcitrant computer.

It's so simple, a ten-year-old could run it, the salesman had promised. Easy for him to say, but Mac was fresh out of ten-year-olds. His secretary and manager had run away together, and he had a crew that was close to mutiny if he didn't figure out how to print their paychecks.

For the last two weeks he'd been withdrawing money from his personal account and giving his employees various sums of cash. According to his last receipt, his funds were about to dry up.

He pressed the enter key.

Beep

"You win," he said, then switched off the machine. There was a twenty-seven-foot sailboat in dry dock because she needed her engine overhauled. Boats he could handle. They weren't filled with beeping drill sergeants, but were living creatures of hand-polished wood. They required attention and a gentle but firm hand . . . kind of like a woman.

He grinned. That line of reasoning had gotten him in trouble more than once. Most of the women he knew bristled at the thought of being "handled." So, he'd stopped telling them his theory. But that didn't change how he felt.

Sailing was his life. He knew the limits of each craft and pushed his ships to the edge, just enough to bend and test, but never to break. Women were the same. "Don't touch" was an enticement, "No trespassing" a guarantee of encroachment. But there was a difference. Boats he was willing to possess, women he only chartered. No long-range commitments for him. He'd had his fill, years before.

Mac stepped out of his office and walked down the ramp to the dock. To the right, the small shipyard and maintenance building were all that remained of a once great shipbuilding company. In the last fifty years,

Spirno Marine had shifted with the economy and become Spirno Charter. Instead of constructing large oceangoing vessels, they now rented boats for fishing and sailing, gave tours of the Keys, and—for a price—provided food and entertainment.

To the left were the slips that housed the two dozen vessels that provided him and his crew with a comfortable, if not extravagant, living. The slips were empty, a good sign in a charter company.

A forty-foot cabin cruiser moved past the jetty. The planks of wood rippled with the motion. Mac automatically shifted his weight; he'd grown up on these docks. He knew every inch of deck, every foot of boat. With his hands on his hips, he surveyed all he owned. And grinned again. Damn, it was *good* to be the king.

"Yo, Mac. What time's the sail this afternoon? You want me to stock the bar?"

He glanced at the lanky young man walking toward him. All neon jams and tank top, Bob was a surfer from California. Despite his six years in Florida, he insisted on talking as if he were fresh off the Zuma Beach sand.

Mac glanced at his watch. "Go ahead and buy the supplies now. I don't expect Mary back with her tour until about three. That should give you time to get the boat ready for the sunset cruise. We're leaving at five."

"All right, man. Anything else?" Bob stood with slumped shoulders and bent knees, as though the act of standing tested the limits of his endurance and at any minute the last of his energy would be used and he'd simply melt to the ground. His red hair stood on end, as if he'd gotten it caught in a propeller, and bright pink zinc oxide protected his nose from the sun.

"That's all, Bob. I'll be in the boathouse looking at the engine."

"I'm outta here. Later, dude."

Amy pulled her car into the parking lot and shut off the motor. Everything ached from her long drive, but she hesitated before stepping out.

The sign above the gate flashed in the afternoon sun. *Spirno Charter*. The script was oddly angled, as though trying to imitate ancient Greek letters. She'd lived in Florida most of her life, had even worked on Nappy's books one summer during college, but this was the first time she'd been to a boat dock.

After opening the door, she slid her legs around and stood up. Her muscles protested the action, but she pushed away the discomfort.

There was so much she'd forgotten.

She breathed deeply and smelled the sea. Salt and ocean and fish and diesel fumes all mingled together into a unique fragrance. She remembered Nappy visiting her with that exact scent clinging to his skin and clothes. When the old man had opened his arms to her, she'd buried her head in his shoulder and hugged him back as hard as she could. He'd been her home port, the familiar lines of his face as welcoming as a beacon light in a storm.

Amy inhaled again. There was something missing. Nappy had also smelled of cigars. She'd always hated the odor, but now she missed it—and him.

A seagull landed on the chain-link fence and scolded her. The bird's screeches mingled with the roar of engines and the incessant clanking of rigging banging against aluminum masts.

"If you're trying to frighten me, don't bother," she said, addressing the bird. "I'm already scared."

The seagull stared at her for another moment; its beady dark eyes never wavered. Then it flapped its wings and moved off, catching a ride on a current of air.

It wasn't too late, she told herself. She could get back into her car and drive until she was clear on the other side of the country. But that would be running away. She'd done enough of that to last a lifetime.

What was he going to say when she told him? she wondered. How angry would he be? There wasn't anything he could do—legally, that is—but his reaction to her decision would make the difference between peaceful coexistence and months of angry confrontation. In the past, he'd always been easygoing, but then she'd never invaded his exclusive domain before.

It's my choice, she reminded herself with a forcefulness that was more bravado than substance. *I've made the decision. No one can change my mind.*

Taking a deep breath, Amy locked the car and started toward the main building. What had been sensible, even casual for work back in Denver, rapidly became inappropriate for Florida. The light-weight blue sweater seemed to attract the sun's rays and magnify them. Her wool pants clung with each step, and the heels of her pumps fit neatly between the planks on the deck.

Bending down for the third time to extract her shoe, she gave up and pulled them both off. So what if she ruined a pair of nylons? It would be a fitting way to end her day.

A man in his early twenties strolled up the walkway. He was tanned and dressed in brightly colored shorts and a tank top, with matching cream on his nose. Amy felt her mouth drop open, and she snapped it shut with an audible sound. Her overactive imagination had been flashing images of her being forced to scale dark fortress walls. She hadn't expected the guard on duty to look like a bit player in a California surfer movie.

"Excuse me, I'm looking for Napoleon . . . ah, Mac Spirno."

The man winked knowingly. "Boss man always did have an eye for bodacious ladies. End of the ramp, that last building." He pointed back the way he'd come. "You coming on the cruise tonight? We've got some totally rad tunes."

"I, ah, I don't think so." Amy smiled tightly and started to move past him.

"Let me know if you change your mind. There's always room for another cool chick, if you know what I mean. You don't surf, do you?"

She choked down her laughter, then glanced back at him. "Not really."

"Wanna learn?"

"No thanks. I get nervous in anything larger than a bathtub."

The man looked disappointed. "Too bad. Later."

"Later," she echoed, then continued moving along the walkway.

The path angled sharply downward. When she reached the dock, the planking changed from solid ground to a restless shifting support, moving endlessly to match the sea. Her leg muscles clenched tightly for balance, Amy walked as close to the wooden railing as possible. The last thing she wanted was an unscheduled dunk in the ocean—or a scheduled dunk, for that matter.

A ski boat skimmed past, stirring up a sizable wake. The wood under her feet began to move up and down, then sideways as the waves hit the shore and returned. She gripped the fence with both hands and held her breath. Only when the rocking had stopped did she let go, one finger at a time. A thin sheet of perspiration covered her back.

Her destination was only ten feet away. The building itself looked solid enough. It hadn't moved at all with the wake from the boat. But between her and safety was an unfenced walkway.

Amy swallowed against the sudden tightening in her throat. It had to be at least two-feet wide. A child could cross it without falling in the water. Step in the center, she told herself. Don't look down, and for heaven's sake, don't look at the ocean.

Six steps. That's all it would take. Six normal steps. Think about something else.

"A man came into a bar," she whispered aloud. "There was a parrot on his shoulder. The bartender looked at the man and—"

The door to the building flung open.

"Bob, could you . . ."

He hadn't changed at all. Well, that wasn't strictly true. Twelve years had passed since her mother had married his father. Twelve years of formal family get-togethers and stiff greetings, during which she'd seen him less than a half-dozen times. But the essence of the man she remembered was the same. And so was her reaction.

His hair was still dark as night—her fingers itched to touch the curls. His eyes still gazed into her soul and made her feel welcome. The lines of his face retained their painfully handsome shape; the new creases only added to his charm.

He'd shaved off the beard five or six years ago. Her mother had been pleased, saying clean shaven he looked less like a pirate. Amy wasn't so sure she agreed. Now, she could see the smooth, strong line of his jaw and the firm but sensual shape of his mouth. Before he'd been handsome and exciting. Now, he was dangerous.

Did he know how she'd dreamed of him? While her friends had pined for rock stars and actors, she'd worshiped at the altar of Mac Spirno. Even after she'd grown up, just the thought of seeing him at a family party had been enough to send her stomach plunging to her toes.

But Mac wasn't into young girls or family obligations. More often than not, he'd called to say he couldn't make it. She hadn't seen him in seven years. He hadn't come to her wedding . . . or Nappy's funeral.

Her eyes drifted down from his face. His body had changed some; he'd filled out. The undeveloped lines of a young adult had been replaced by the hard-muscled strength of a man who worked—physically worked—for a living.

A cropped T-shirt, faded and bleached by the sun, clung tenaciously to his chest. There was a band of muscled, tanned skin bisected by a narrowing line of dark hair, then denim cut-offs settled on narrow hips. The fabric had been worn so many times the shape of his body was molded into the cloth.

She licked her lips nervously and glanced back at his face. The smile was as she remembered. Warm and friendly, with only a hint of the devil, it flashed white against his tan.

"Amy? Is that you?" He held open his arms.

"Hi." She raised her hand in greeting, but kept her distance.

She'd driven from Denver to southern Florida in the dead of winter to beard the lion in his den. Well, here was the lion, but she stood as still as a deer caught in headlights. All her brave talk of taking charge became meaningless. From the moment they'd met, Mac'd had the power to render her speechless and immobile. Some things never changed.

"Hi? That's it? I don't think so, Amy."

Mac moved forward and caught her in a bear hug. Her purse and shoes fell from her hands as strong arms locked around her ribs and lifted her from the ground. She had always thought of herself as tall, all long legs with nowhere to put them, but around Mac, she felt petite and feminine. He was six-feet-four inches of pure brawn.

As he spun her around, she clutched at his shoulders. The world tilted; there was the building, then shore, then ocean. She closed her eyes and let his strength seep into her being and energize her. His skin carried the scent of the sea. For a moment, she was tempted to let her lips press against the side of his neck to see if he tasted salty.

Her eyes flew open. What was she thinking? Mac was her *brother*. Okay, so he was really her step-brother, but that didn't change anything.

He stopped turning, but didn't release her. Amy became aware of their bodies pressed together, from chest to knee. The thin layers of their clothing weren't enough to stop the transfer of heat. Her fingers lost themselves in his hair and she leaned even closer. For the first time in years, she felt safe, alive . . . and wanting.

Mac told himself to let go. What had started as a friendly embrace had ignited into something more. But Amy felt too good, too right. Still, *she* probably didn't appreciate his enthusiastic greeting. Releasing his hold, he let her slip slowly to earth. Her body slid against his, sending shock waves through his system.

The slow fire licked against him . . . once . . . twice . . . then settled into a steady burn. They stood far enough apart that he couldn't feel warmth from her, but he knew it was there. When the hell had Amy grown up?

Her hands still rested on his shoulders, but she was looking straight ahead, as if the shape of his bottom lip was fascinating. Maybe it was, but he doubted that was why she refused to look him in the eye. He debated the wisdom of apologizing for what had just happened, then realized nothing had—except in his suddenly fertile imagination. Better to ignore the fact that he was thinking very un-fraternal thoughts.

"You cut your hair," he said finally, picking the safest observation from all that came to mind.

She raised her chin and glanced at him. "About three years ago."

Had her eyes always been that color? he wondered. Somewhere between blue and indigo? They were the exact shade of the ocean just after a storm, when the surface waves were calm but turbulence lingered below. Her long lashes swept down and hid her thoughts from him.

He touched her head. The long blonde braid had been sheared in favor of a short, layered style. He liked the way the hair fell across her forehead, but left her ears bare. She had perfect shell-shaped ears. One finger traced the delicate crease.

A blush stole across her smooth cheeks and she ducked away. "Stop that. You're tickling me." She moved back about two feet, then glanced over her shoulder at the ocean. Swallowing, she took a step closer to him. "Well, I'm here."

"So, you are."

When she wasn't smiling, her mouth relaxed into a perfect cupid's bow. The lower lip was full, almost pouty.

Mac coughed suddenly. His thoughts were way out of line. He'd invited Amy to come to Florida for a working vacation. In the next seven days, she was supposed to rest up, get some sun, sign a few papers, then go back to Denver. Seduction wasn't part of the plan.

He dropped a kiss on the top of her head, ignoring her scent, his desire, and the fire flickering between them. "Come on, kid. I'll give you the nickel tour."

Amy allowed Mac to lead her up the wide gangplank and into the office. While she stood in the center of the messy room and blinked to adjust to the less-bright interior, he flipped on the air conditioning, then pulled two sodas out of the small refrigerator in the corner.

"Thanks." She took the can and glanced around the large office.

Three desks formed an uneven U. Stacks of papers covered every available surface, including an overflowing box in the center of the cement floor. Rigging, oars, and ropes competed for space in the far corner. A long window ran along one wall; a glimpse of the marina made her stomach clench uncomfortably.

Why this? she wondered for the hundredth time. Why couldn't Nappy have owned a hardware store or a feed lot? Why did she have to hate the water so much? But that didn't matter. She'd made her decision. She was taking charge of her life . . . starting sometime in the next few minutes.

"Have a seat."

Mac motioned for her to find a place on the cracked green vinyl sofa opposite the view, while he perched on a corner of one of the desks. One bare leg stretched to the floor, the other was bent at the knee and swung back and forth.

Looking away from tanned skin covering muscled thigh, she moved a tackle box to the floor, then perched on the slippery plastic. "You really shouldn't have gone to so much trouble for little old me."

He shrugged. "No trouble."

"Yeah. I see that. Has this building always been on the verge of being condemned?"

"What are you talking about? This place has charm."

"Oh." She grinned. "You must point it out to me sometime."

He chuckled and held her gaze. There was that damn lazy smile again, she thought grimly. It worked on her now as well as it had when she'd been a teen-ager. Irritation flashed through her body, giving her the courage to begin her speech. "When we spoke on the phone, you said you wanted to talk about the partnership agreement."

"That's right." He took a long swallow of his drink and set the can on the desk. "I need you to sign some papers, maybe take a look at the books. We're not doing too badly. As I mentioned before, the company bought several boats last year, so the cash flow is tight every month, but I think we'll make it.'' He shrugged. ''Hope you weren't counting on a big bonus to buy a fur coat to keep you warm in Denver.''

''I don't wear fur,'' she said automatically. ''Mac, I . . .'' She cleared her throat. ''You mentioned your office manager had eloped. Any news?''

''Yeah, but not the good kind. Bill and Sally aren't coming back. I'm going to look for a couple new bodies next week.''

''That won't be necessary.''

''Why?''

Forcing herself to meet the suddenly wary expression in his eyes, she spoke. ''I'm not going to be a silent partner any longer, Mac. I'm moving back to Florida to work in the business.''

For a big man, he moved fast. In less than a heartbeat, he had sprung to his feet and crossed the room. When he was inches from her knees, he stopped and planted his hands on his hips. ''You're kidding.''

''I wish I was,'' she said, more to herself than him. ''It's been nine months since Nappy died and left us both the company. I've been doing a lot of thinking and I want to be a real partner. It's not fair that you do all the work and I get half the money.''

Mac turned away and paced to the window. ''That's a dumb idea. So far, there hasn't been any money. Besides, what do you know about boats? The occasional weekend cruise hardly qualifies you as an expert.'' He glanced at the pale sweater she wore. ''I can't picture you tuning up an engine in your fancy clothes.''

"You still need an office manager. I have a degree in business.''

"What do you know about office work?''

"I worked on the books one summer.''

He raised an eyebrow. "We've gone high-tech in the last few years. I doubt anything you learned ten years ago still applies. Can you run a payroll program, balance books, or even order supplies?''

He had her there. Her first job out of college had been arranged by her mother. The title of executive assistant had turned out to mean chief errand runner and queen of the coffeepot. In Denver, she had been in charge of coordinating volunteer services at the city's zoo. Neither had offered her much experience in the logistics of running an office, but she had graduated near the top of her class. Surely, Florida's premier business school had taught her something useful. Even if it hadn't, she wasn't afraid of hard work.

"Mac, I'm aware of my limitations, but you can't scare me away with your scowls. I'm still your partner. I mean to make a fresh start. If you don't want to work with me, then buy me out and I'll go somewhere else.''

He faced the window. "I can't do that. All the capital is tied up in the new boats. I wouldn't be able to get another loan for at least six months.''

The tension in his back made her want to go to him and soothe away his troubles, but right now, she *was* his trouble. The silence stretched on.

Should she try and explain? she wondered. Tell him what it was like to have every moment of her life carefully planned by others? Would he understand what had driven her to run away and try to start over? That in the end, she had realized she had to come back and stand on her own and claim what was hers—to defeat those who doubted, prove to those who would not believe—to prove to herself that she was strong?

By virtue of an inheritance, her journey began on this boat dock. Mac could help along the way or prove to be a stumbling block, but he wasn't going to keep her from making the trip.

"The old man always had a soft spot for you," he said finally. "I still miss him."

The old man in question wasn't Mac's father, she knew, but his paternal grandfather, Nappy.

"Me, too." Her voice was barely a whisper.

Even after all this time, it was hard to imagine that she'd never see Nappy again. He'd been the only one who cared about her. On parents' day at her various boarding schools, Nappy had always been the first to arrive and the last to leave. He'd loved her. Losing him had been harder than losing her husband . . . almost as hard as losing her baby.

"When he left the business to both of us, I think I knew someday you'd come and claim your half." Anger and resignation battled in his voice.

She set her can of soda on the floor and rose to her feet. After stepping into her shoes, she crossed the cement floor and stood next to him.

"Why now?" he asked.

Mac watched as Amy glanced down at the floor, then over at the desk, anything to avoid his eyes or looking out the window. She wasn't exactly dying to spend her life at sea, he thought. In fact, he couldn't remember ever seeing her at the docks. He'd always known women were stubborn, but this was crazy. He ought to tell her no and let the cards fall where they may.

Then she smiled slightly; the gentle curve of her full lips made his irritation drain away.

"I'm taking charge of my life," she said. The blue of her eyes darkened to a midnight sky.

He read the flash of pain, and understood the cause. There were memories he didn't share, but could imagine.

"Everybody's always told me what to do," she said. "I'm tired of it. Nappy left half this business to me. No one has the right to take that away from me, not even you."

He glanced at his shirt, half expecting to see a dagger sticking out of his heart. He'd always been a sucker for the underdog. It had been one of the few qualities he'd been proud of—now it was being used against him. Tell her to go away, he told himself.

The instruction lacked conviction. He was going under for the third time and there wasn't a damn thing he could do to save himself.

"I applaud your new-found strength," he said. "Forgive me for wishing you'd picked someone else's life to disrupt."

"You could consider it an honor."

She looked as young and vulnerable as she had the first time he'd met her. He'd known his father was marrying a woman with three daughters, but the information had been meaningless. Locked in a struggle to be his own man, Mac hadn't thought of them as people until Nappy had pulled a picture of Amy out of his wallet. The small photo, taken her first year in high school, had highlighted her fragile beauty, the tentative quality behind her sweet smile. The old man had spoken of her with affection and love. His thick Greek accent gave the words added formality—she was the daughter he'd never had, the granddaughter he'd always hoped for. Mac could no more send her away than he could turn his back on all the old man had taught him.

But he didn't have to like it. He loved women, their soft voices and softer bodies. The way they walked and laughed and smiled. But he didn't trust them . . . or her. Jenny had taught him that.

His fingers trailed down her face to cup her jaw. She was tall, almost five eight, but seemed small next to him. The stubborn set of her mouth told its own story. It didn't matter that she was about as intimidating as a kitten, she'd fight to the end for what she wanted.

Mac could stand up to the world, and had on several occasions, but he'd always had a soft spot for Amy. And he'd never been able to resist his grandfather. For all of his thirty-five years, he'd been accused of being the black sheep of the family, only doing what *he* wanted to do. Yet here he was, ready to turn his world upside down on the say-so of one young woman and the wishes of a dead man.

"I suppose you ran all this by a lawyer?" he asked. She nodded.

"And I don't have a choice about letting you work your half?"

"Not really," she whispered.

He dropped his hand and moved to the desk. "Then let's get some ground rules established. You are in charge of the office, and only the office. The boats are my responsibility. I don't come into your space and you don't come into mine. Do you understand?"

"Yes." She tucked her hands into her front pockets. "What else?"

The relief in her eyes would have been amusing if his gut hadn't chosen that minute to tie itself in a knot. "In six months we re-evaluate the situation. If it's not working out, we get a bank loan and I buy you out. Fair enough?"

She moved closer to the desk. "And if it is?"

"Give me a break."

"Come on, Mac. It'll be fun working together. What's the worst that could happen?"

The worst? He could forget his rule about not mixing business and pleasure, as well as the notion he'd always held that Amy was his little sister. Apparently his soft spot for her had moved to his head, because he was standing there thinking things he had no right to think.

Was she quiet in bed, holding back and hiding her response to passion? Did she burn with a fire that threatened to consume a man in a fiery death on his way to heaven? He'd never find out. No woman was going to change the way he played the game. So why did he have a sinking feeling that the consummate playboy had just been played for a fool?

TWO

Amy pressed her foot down on the accelerator and eased her car forward. Several yards ahead, Mac signaled his turn and rode his motorcycle out of the parking lot. In twelve years, that too had stayed the same. She couldn't really imagine him in a regular vehicle. There was something about Napoleon Christopher Spirno that required the power, the freedom of a bike. Even now, dressed casually in shorts and a T-shirt, he was as much a part of the machine as the engine itself.

While they drove south on the highway, she sensed the slow dissipation of the day's frustrations. Tension left her shoulders—only to be replaced by a subtle but insistent craving deep in her chest. Just watching the wide expanse of his back, the way his leg muscles bunched then released as he changed gears, the sun reflecting off the black helmet that protected him was enough to make her knees tremble.

Get a grip, she told herself. He was just a man.

She sighed. Those simple words didn't begin to explain the complexities of her stepbrother. There was something about being with Mac that made her feel alive . . . close to the edge. He was the only person she knew who did exactly what he wanted. No compromises, no regrets.

Even before they'd met, she'd listened to his father, the judge, complain about his only son's stubborn resolve. The youngest Spirno hadn't wanted to read the law; his life was boats and the ocean. She'd envied his ability to do exactly what he wanted. She still did.

They moved off the highway and onto the residential street. Amy tapped her fingers against the steering wheel. She recognized the wide road with the large, secluded houses set well back from the sidewalks. When Mac had said he'd help her get settled, she'd thought he'd take her to a hotel. Instead, they were traveling the familiar path to Nappy's house . . . the house the old man had left to Mac.

She pulled into the cobblestone driveway and watched while he parked the bike, then removed his helmet. It was almost four o'clock. The sun was starting its daily descent. The tall palm trees in front of the Spanish-style home cast long shadows on the driveway. As Mac hooked the helmet on the bike, then swung his leg over the seat and stood up, he moved from light, to dark, and back to light. The ever-changing pattern made him seem mysterious . . . and very male.

A small shiver began in Amy's stomach. Two parts concern, one part anticipation. If she totaled all the time she'd spent with Mac in the last twelve years, it wouldn't add up to more than a week. She couldn't stay here with him . . . alone.

He sauntered over to the car. His arm swept wide to encompass the grounds. "What do you think?"

She opened the door and stepped outside. Nappy had kept the front yard bare, with only grass and the tall palms for relief. Mac had turned the narrow space between the circular drive and the white-stuccoed building into a garden of color and fragrance. Calla lilies reflected the light, while Japanese irises rose tall above them. Low to the ground, pansies poked up their yellow and purple faces, as though waiting to be noticed.

"It's very, ah, nice," she managed finally. "Why did you bring me here? I thought I could check into a motel or something."

His dark eyes met hers. A flash of resentment sliced through her as she took in his dark lashes. Guys didn't need long lashes. She, however, was stuck with short skimpy ones that required a minimum of two coats of mascara every morning.

Just then, he smiled. It was the heart-wrenching sort of smile that caused the lines by his temples to crinkle and deepen, and the top of the dimple on his cheek to make an appearance. What would it be like to be the center of Mac Spirno's universe?

"You'd agreed to stay here for your visit," he said as he took her arm and led her toward the front door. "Why don't we stick to that plan."

She paused in midstep. "For six months? Won't I be in the way?"

"I make it a rule never to have toga parties at my house."

"Please! You know what I meant. Besides . . ." She had a feeling that guilt was written all over her face. "You have every right to be angry. I did sort of barge

in on the business. You're being very nice, but . . ."
She swallowed. "What I'm trying to say is . . ."

"It's all right. I know what you're trying to say. I'm
not angry. Stunned, perhaps, maybe even intrigued."
He shrugged. "I worked with Nappy my whole life.
The idea of a partner is hardly shocking. Besides, it's
too much work to hold a grudge."

His dark eyes were surprisingly clear of shadows.
Mac wasn't kidding. He might not like the change in
circumstances, but he wasn't going to make her life
hell simply to punish her. The last knot of apprehension
came untied and she sighed.

"I kind of like the idea of a roommate," he said as
he pulled her up the path. "The house is huge. I'm
constantly getting lost and I never remember to buy
groceries. It'll be nice to argue over who gets the com-
ics in the Sunday paper. Sometimes I get tired of being
alone."

His voice had deepened with each word until the last
one came out with a husky, hungry sound. She glanced
at him, but his expression gave nothing away. Maybe
she'd imagined the insinuation in his tone. The drive
had been long and tiring. The fact that his hand, resting
just above her elbow, incited a small riot in her nerve
endings was merely an incidental piece of information.

He unlocked the door and pushed it open. As she
walked into the cool foyer, Mac stepped in behind her.
"Close your eyes," he said.

"What?" She tried to turn around, but he was too
close. If she moved any direction but forward, they'd
touch. Her heart had already had its aerobic workout
today, thanks to him.

"Close your eyes. I want to show you something."

"They're closed."

"Tell me what you remember when you think of this house."

An involuntary smile curled her lips. "Nappy. He always brought me here on the weekends. We'd play chess in the library. I'd read by the pool." She swallowed against the sudden pressure of tears. "Some of my happiest memories are in this house."

"Exactly."

He breathed the word in her ear. Now that they were away from the ocean, she could smell his cologne. The spicy, masculine scent made her think of tangled sheets and icy champagne.

"E—exactly what?"

"Why would you want to stay in a hotel when I'm offering you a few months in a place that makes you feel comfortable? Would you rather stay with your mother?"

Mac chuckled softly when Amy opened her eyes and glared at him over her shoulder. "Don't even ask," she said.

He leaned against the wall and watched her walk into the living area. The changes he'd made were relatively minor. Would she approve?

Like most homes in Florida, Nappy'd had his built to be open and airy. The main room was a large square that consisted of living and family areas, along with the kitchen and dining room. Three-foot partitions, covered in the same creamy matte wallpaper as the walls, divided the space. Two wings jutted out at right angles. His bedroom was to the left, Amy's would be on the right.

In the living room, Mac had replaced the ancient

leather chairs with long modern sofas. Some of the paintings were his, as was the bronze Remington sculpture that rested on the glass coffee table.

Amy walked around slowly. Her high-heels clicked on the black and white marble floor. She stopped next to the wooden figurehead in the far corner.

"I used to make up stories about her," she said softly. One finger touched the carved hair flowing down the back of the half-naked mermaid. "I pretended that she was my long-lost sister and would come and take me back to her magic kingdom under the sea." She smiled sheepishly. "The only problem with the fantasy is my dislike of the ocean."

Mac's heart constricted at her words. She had no way of knowing that troubled vulnerability darkened her blue eyes to navy, and caused the corner of her perfect lips to tremble slightly. He wanted to hold her in his arms and promise that she'd never be lonely again.

He frowned. Since when did he run around rescuing women? His methods leaned more toward a charming but unrelenting assault, then a victory celebration that often lasted for days. But Amy wasn't his usual sophisticated type. Life had knocked her around some and she'd never developed an armor tough enough to hide the scars.

"She did mention that she'd missed you," he said teasingly. "Come on, stay here."

"For six months? I don't know what to say."

"How about yes?" For a reason he refused to analyze, it was very important that he keep Amy under close supervision. Probably just his conscience kicking in to take Nappy's place, he told himself. It couldn't mean anything else. "What's the worst that could happen?" he asked, repeating her earlier question.

Her gaze met his. Instead of giving a teasing response, she was silent. Awareness flashed across her face, then disappeared, but he knew what she'd been thinking. As he'd already figured out, little Amy wasn't so little after all.

He straightened up and walked toward her. A need to possess, to claim what would be his, slowed his step to a swagger. Hot, heavy desire began to bubble and flow.

She stepped back, then crossed her arms across her chest. The protective gesture told him volumes. She was afraid . . . and not just of him. He frowned. Ten minutes alone with her and he'd already forgotten his own rule of no involvement.

He stuck his hands in his back pockets and came to a stop about a foot in front of her. There were dark smudges under her eyes and a tired droop to her shoulders. He touched her nose with his right index finger. "Come on, princess. Let's get you settled."

In a flash, the predatory, very male Mac had been replaced by the charming stepbrother she'd known for years. Amy didn't know if she was feeling relief or regret. It was too soon to analyze the emotion.

"I haven't said I was staying yet."

"So, you haven't." He rested his weight on the balls of his feet and rocked slowly back and forth. "Well?"

She glanced at the polished marble floor, then back at him. "My mother will probably come to visit." Lynn and Mac had never been more than uneasy acquaintances. The smallest incident could, and often did, escalate into full-scale battle.

Mac frowned. "I'm a grown man. I think I'll survive. The question is, can you stay here, knowing she won't want you to?"

"Of course, I can. I'm all grown up, too."

She hated the doubt she saw in his eyes, but there was no denying the truth. She *had* spent most of her life doing exactly what her mother advised. It was only in the last two years that she'd started making her own decisions. Independence was coming slowly, and at a price.

"What room am I in?" she asked.

"The one you always used when you visited Nappy. I, ah, took the liberty of ordering some new furniture. If you don't like it, I can get something else."

She raised an eyebrow. "I'm not sure if I should be insulted or flattered."

"At what?"

"The take-charge attitude."

"You're the one who wants to be partners. There's still time to back out."

"Not a chance, sailor. What about you? Are you up to answering to someone else?"

He shrugged. "I told you before. I'll admit you've thrown me for a loop, but I'm not going to be a jerk about it. You are half owner of the business. I'd rather work with someone I like, than fight with an adversary. Besides, in six months you'll be begging me to buy you out."

She smiled. "You sound very sure of yourself. Do you always get everything you want?"

He winked. "Of course. I'm a helluva guy. I'm surprised you haven't already noticed."

Amy made a gagging noise. "I'm too busy being awed by your conceit."

"Never conceit. Confidence. There's a difference."

Yup, he was right, she thought. Conceit would have made him insufferable—confidence made him irresistible. She walked down the hall, pausing briefly to stare at the wall. Pictures covered the painted expanse. From floor to ceiling, family photographs looked back at her. But these weren't the formal portraits that graced her mother's and sisters' houses. These were candid shots showing a young Nappy, standing tall and proud in his Navy uniform. Photos of Mac's parents butted up against her own relatives. There was a shot of her with Nappy a couple of years before the wedding. She must have been about fourteen. She'd been a skinny bean pole with braces and straight blonde hair. The love in the old man's face caused a tear to slip down her cheek.

"Who did this?"

"I did." Mac brushed his thumb across her face. "Hey, I thought you'd like it. Don't cry."

She sniffed. "I'm not. And I do like it. Where did you find the pictures?"

"There was a box of them in Nappy's study. I went through them and picked out the ones I liked. The rest are still around if you want to have a look."

"Okay. Maybe later."

She stepped into the bedroom. The juvenile wallpaper had been replaced with a pale rose print with the pattern continued in the bedspread. White wicker furniture made the room seem like a patio garden. The effect was restful and elegant.

"Mac, it's a beautiful room. I love it. Thank you."

He was standing just inside the doorway. One shoulder leaned against the wall as though he held up the building. She moved toward him and raised on her toes to brush a kiss on his cheek. Her lids started to flutter closed. At the last second, he turned his head and her lips squarely planted on his.

Too shocked to do anything but register the sensation of his warm, tempting mouth, she remained exactly in position. Her eyes flew open and she saw the amusement on his face.

Embarrassment settled in. She took a hurried step back and nearly tripped when her hip connected painfully with the corner of the wicker dresser. Stop it, she told herself. She was acting like a girl with her first crush. Smiling tightly, she eased away from his overpowering presence, then came to a halt in the middle of the room.

Mac *was* her first crush. He was her only crush. If her heart tap dancing against her ribs was any indication, her feelings hadn't changed all that much. Why? she wanted to scream. After all these years she couldn't possibly still have feelings for him. Could she?

The man in question offered her a lazy smile. "I'll bring in your luggage."

"Luggage?"

"Yeah. Those bags in the trunk of your car?"

"Oh. Sure, thanks. Here." She pulled the keys from her pants pocket and handed them to him.

He didn't move. "I have to go back to the marina. There's a sunset cruise leaving in half an hour and I'm the captain. I've left plenty of food in the fridge. Sylvia, the cleaning lady, comes three times a week. She does the laundry, too, so leave it out for her." He ran a hand through his dark hair. "I think that about covers everything. Do you have any questions?"

"Questions?"

He grinned. "I'll take that as a no. You'd better unpack and get some rest, Amy. As a working partner, you're expected to be at work bright and early in the morning."

She touched her fingers to her still-tingling lips. "I'll be ready."

Amy stretched on the bed and rolled to look at the clock radio on the wicker night stand. The red numbers glowed in the dark room. Eleven-forty? It couldn't be. She'd closed her eyes for only a second, but that had been a little after five.

She stood up and glanced around the room. One suitcase was already empty and standing neatly in the corner. The other three waited patiently by the door. A grumble from her stomach was a reminder that she hadn't eaten since she'd stopped for a quick burger at noon. The first order of business was a shower, then food, then maybe unpacking.

After digging through one of the bags to find her shampoo, she stumbled into the bathroom and turned on the water. Twenty minutes later, she pulled on a clean oversized T-shirt. The soft cotton fell to mid-thigh. Her robe was in one of the suitcases, but Amy decided she could risk a trip to the kitchen. She vaguely remembered hearing Mac come in a couple of hours ago. No doubt he was already in bed.

She opened her door and stepped into the hall. One light from the living room illuminated her way. As she passed by the pictures on the wall, Amy glanced again at the display. A picture of Nappy as a young man made her smile. He'd been handsome with strong features. Mac took after him.

She moved closer and looked for a picture of her wedding; there weren't any. Nor were there any photos of her ex-husband or Mac's ex-wife. She remembered several Christmases ago when the confident brunette had talked knowledgeably to Mac's father about cases and briefs and criminal law. Amy had sat in the corner and envied her poise.

She shook her head and walked purposefully toward the kitchen. No looking back, she reminded herself.

The refrigerator offered an assortment of treats. She cut off a thick wedge of cheese and selected a bunch of grapes, then poured herself a glass of sparkling water. When her snack was prepared, she walked to the back patio and pushed open the sliding glass door.

The night air was still and fragrant. The sound of the ocean rushing to the shore provided relaxing background noise. A rectangular screen kept out the bugs while allowing the moonlight to filter down and settle in the pool. Anthuriums, their red blooms glowing like hot, melted wax, defined the perimeter of the backyard. To her right was a table and several lounge chairs. Amy set her plate on the table and turned to fluff up a cushion. She shrieked when her thigh came in contact with something warm and alive and strong.

"Mac?"

"I was wondering how long you were going to ignore me."

As her eyes grew accustomed to the dimness, she saw him sprawled on a chaise lounge next to the pool. His features were blurred, only the flash of white when he smiled told her his mood. He was still wearing shorts, but the T-shirt had been replaced by a short-sleeved buttoned shirt that hung open. The light-colored fabric reflected the moonlight and cast shadows on his chest.

"I thought you'd gone to bed. I didn't mean to disturb you."

"You're not disturbing me. In fact, I could use a little company."

His hand captured hers and he pulled her down beside him. Her hip pushed against his knee. She turned to face him, but jumped when their thighs touched.

"Feel better?" he asked. "I checked on you before I left, but you were already asleep."

His hand still held hers. The brush of his thumb across her palm sent shivery sensations up her arm and through her body. Amy realized she was wearing nothing but bikini panties and a T-shirt. Pulling back, she crossed her arms over her chest.

"I guess I was more tired than I thought."

"Yeah. You were snoring away, dead to the world."

She glared at him. "I don't snore."

She caught the flash of white as he grinned. "How do you know? Maybe your lovers are just being polite."

Lovers? Her? A laugh of disbelief hovered in her throat, but she held it back. If she counted that fling in college and her ex-husband, she could legitimately use the plural form of the word.

"Maybe you're just teasing me."

Mac picked up the bottle of beer beside him and took a sip. "Are you telling me you have absolute proof you don't snore?"

She didn't dignify his question with an answer, choosing instead to stand up and retrieve her late-night meal. She started to sit on the far side of the table, but he pulled a chair close to his and patted the seat invitingly.

"Come on. I won't bite."

Mac wondered if Amy would stay where she was, but after several seconds she picked up her plate and settled next to him. The subdued lighting blurred the edges of everything in the patio, yet he could see the shapely, feminine lines of her calves. His gaze moved upwards. The plate balanced delicately on her lap. The soft folds of her nightshirt hid most of her midsection from view, but the rise and fall of her breasts was unmistakable. With each breath, the full curves moved up; the barest hint of her nipples pushing against the cloth teased at him. Was the echo of arousal due to the night . . . her mood . . . or to him?

"Want a grape?" She held out a bunch to him.

"Sure."

Mac set the beer bottle on the patio and leaned forward. Instead of grabbing the fruit with his hand, he plucked one with his teeth. The corner of his mouth brushed against Amy's finger.

Indigo eyes met and held his own. He heard the intake of air, felt the sizzling spark of fire, and wondered why the hell he was playing a game he had no intention of completing. He settled back in the chair.

"Want to talk about your luggage?" he asked.

"W—what do you mean?"

The quiver in her voice caused a very satisfied heat somewhere around his crotch. "I brought in the suitcases, but you've got several boxes still in the backseat.

I didn't know what they were or what you were planning to do with them, so I left them in the car. Looks like you were planning to stay even if I'd fought you on the partnership.''

She made a great show of setting her plate on the table and drinking from her glass. The silence grew longer, but Mac simply waited. Fishing had taught him patience; there was no point in reeling in the line if there was nothing on the other end.

''Yes.'' She sounded as though she were waiting for him to yell at her.

He sat up and scooted to the end of the chaise lounge. When he was in front of her, he took her small hands in his and held them tightly. ''Amy, I'm not your mother. I have no burning need to run your life. I have enough problems with my own. If you want to go live with the elephants in Africa, I'd be happy to come visit. Instead, you've chosen to stay here. That's okay. You're a grown woman, as you reminded me this afternoon. You don't have to answer to anyone.''

''I'm not like you,'' she whispered. ''Mother always told me what to do, and she was usually right. But you . . . you've done whatever you wanted. How did you find the courage?''

He shrugged. ''I don't know, princess. I just do what my gut tells me is right. Sometimes it's hard, sometimes I make mistakes. There's no magic. It's called living.''

Her hair fell across her forehead. He gave in to the temptation and brushed it back.

Soft. The silky blonde strands gleaming like silver were so damn soft. His other hand reached up to cup her jaw. Her mouth parted slightly. Dark lashes, still spiky from sleep, drifted shut against her cheek. When the pointed tip of her pink tongue slipped out to moisten her bottom lip, he felt the blood rush to his groin. Even the ocean grew silent in anticipation.

He remembered he hadn't had a woman since before Nappy had died; he remembered the feel of Amy's body against his when he'd held her that afternoon; he remembered her shocked look when he'd teased her about having lovers; he remembered the adoration in her eyes; he remembered the kiss in her bedroom.

He touched the tip of her nose with his finger, then released her. "The down side of doing what I wanted was the years my father and I fought. At least you've never been the black sheep of the family."

She stared at him for several seconds, then blinked. He wanted to kiss away the confusion, but that would only lead to what he was trying so very hard to avoid.

"But you reconciled," she said.

"It took about ten years. That's a long time to stay mad at someone."

"Is that why you rarely came to family gatherings?"

He stood up and nodded. "It was easier than fighting with my dad. You know how stubborn the judge can be."

Amy grinned and looked at Mac. "Yeah. About as stubborn as you."

He feigned being shot and staggered a few steps. "I'm wounded you would think so little of me."

"I can tell."

She watched as he collected the dishes and carried them back into the kitchen. His off-key humming drifted back to her and she giggled. When the laugh turned into a yawn, she rose and stretched.

"Getting sleepy?" he asked as he stepped onto the patio and walked to the table.

"Yes. I think I'll unpack a little, then turn in."

"What do you want to do about those boxes?"

"Can you store them in the garage?"

"Sure. Where's your furniture?"

Amy looked down and rubbed her toe against the leg of the chair. "I don't have any."

"What?"

"All the stuff Nappy gave me is in storage here. The apartment in Denver was furnished."

"Didn't you have a house full when you were married?"

She nodded, still unable to look up.

"What happened to it?"

"I gave it to Ted," she mumbled, then waited for the explosion. Her mother had been furious. Her sisters had gone to great lengths to point out that the furniture was community property. Even the judge had been disappointed.

"Because you wanted to forget?" Mac asked.

"Yes." She glanced at him. "How did you know?"

"Makes perfect sense to me. And yes, I'll be happy to store your stuff in the garage."

"I've got a few more things being shipped down here."

"No problem."

"Well, I guess I'll go in now." She waited, hoping he would ask her to stay with him, but he only smiled. "Good night."

"Night, Amy."

With her hand on the door, she started to enter the house, then paused. "Mac?"

"Yeah?"

"Why aren't there any pictures of Ted and Jenny on the wall?" She heard the chair being pushed back against the table, but didn't turn around.

"I didn't think either of us would want to be reminded of our ex-spouses. Was I wrong?"

"No." She paused. "Mac?"

"Yes, Amy?"

"Why didn't you come to my wedding?" She hated the hurt that echoed in the words, but it was too late to call the question back.

"You didn't come to mine," he answered.

She spun and found him standing directly behind her. "You eloped."

"Oh, I forgot. Well, I *was* at your wedding."

"I didn't see you."

"I was there." He put his hands on his hips. "Don't you believe me?"

She shook her head. "Prove it."

"Let's see. There was a bunch of people. You were married in the church by my dad's house. What else? Oh, you wore white."

She groaned. "I should have known what answer I'd get from a man like you."

"What are you talking about? I'm incredibly charming."

"So you keep reminding me." The problem being . . . he was absolutely correct. He was also attractive, enticing, and completely convinced she was still a child.

Mac gave her a quick hug, then moved back to the pool. "Go on in. I'm going to swim a few laps."

"Now?"

"Yes, now. Unless you have something else you need to know?" He shrugged out of his shirt and tossed it on the lounge chair. The light of the moon turned his skin to a molten gold. The hollows and bulges created when he stretched made him seem like a living sculpture. Dark hair, gleaming like curls of onyx, swirled down his chest in an ever-narrowing pattern, then disappeared into the waistband of his shorts.

Why did he keep treating her like a teenager? She could have sworn that he was going to kiss her, really kiss her, earlier. But he'd brushed off the chance and left her feeling like a fool. Learn the lesson, she told herself. He's into confident overachievers, not heartbroken waifs who don't have a clue about life or men.

"No more inquiries," she murmured, suddenly mesmerized by the way his hand was unzipping his shorts.

"Amy?"

"Yes?" She couldn't tear her eyes away from the metal tab moving lower and lower.

"I didn't bring a suit out with me."

"So?" She caught her breath as his words sunk in. "Oh. I was just . . . Oh! Good night."

The sound of his laughter followed her down the hall and into her bedroom.

THREE

Amy adjusted her earrings and stood in front of the mirror. The outfit she'd chosen for her first day of work at Spirno Charter was a navy and white short-sleeved dress. The buttons parading down the front had small anchors on them. Very nautical, she thought to herself as she slipped into her navy flats. Professional and businesslike, with just the smallest touch of whimsy.

After a last flick of the brush on her short hair, she stepped into the hall. The smell of coffee and something sweet and cinnamon caused her to hurry.

The kitchen was mercifully empty. After last night's encounter, she wasn't looking forward to another session with Mac. He had the ability to wind her up, then let the spring go and watch her spin in circles. If only he weren't so charming . . . and good looking . . . and friendly. She sighed. It was like asking a puppy not to be cute.

She poured the coffee into a cup and took a sip.

Heaven. Leaning against the counter, Amy stared out into the backyard. In the light of morning, the patio with its table and chairs looked deceptively innocent. Who could have guessed that a few short hours ago Mac had touched her face and taunted her with the promise of his kiss . . . only to pull away. The man was a tease.

She laughed as she sent a mental apology to all the guys in high school who had complained when she wasn't willing to indulge in a petting session in the back of their cars.

"You're in a cheerful mood this morning. The ocean air must agree with you."

Amy willed herself not to turn and look at him. Just the sound of Mac's voice, still husky with sleep, was enough to send shivers colliding along her spine. "It's good to be back," she said, proud of the calm inflection of her words.

"I see you're dressed for a day at the office. I'm impressed."

"Thank you."

Mac strolled in front of her and leaned against the counter. A white T-shirt bearing the Greek-style letters of the charter company's logo was stretched tightly across his broad shoulders. Light blue shorts clung to narrow hips. The rest of him was bare. She gulped her coffee and coughed when the hot liquid burned her throat.

"Are you all right?"

"Fine," she said weakly. "It just went down the wrong way." She coughed again. "Really, I'm fine."

He nodded solemnly, but his dark eyes laughed at her. The tiny creases at the corners deepened, even though his firm lips remained perfectly straight. Her eyes dropped to the pulse in his throat, just visible above the T-shirt. The slow beat mocked the rapid thumping in her own chest.

"Amy?"

"Hmm?" She looked back at his face.

"You look very pretty this morning."

His compliment brought a blush to her cheeks. Heat climbed steadily up to her hair line. "Thank you."

"Very businesslike."

There was something in his tone that warned her all was not well. "But?"

He leaned forward and whispered in her ear, "You're going to a boat dock, not an insurance office."

She slid along the counter to escape the soft puffs of air tickling her neck. "I wanted to look appropriate."

"How about looking as if you're having a good time?"

"Meaning I should change into something more casual?"

"Wouldn't hurt. I'm sure you don't want to intimidate the staff on your first day of work."

A timer went off and she stepped aside when Mac grabbed a potholder and opened the oven. Steaming cinnamon rolls, baked to a golden brown, made her mouth water.

"I didn't know you cooked," she said.

His grin was pure male. "There's a lot about me you don't know, princess. But we've got all the time in the world for you to learn."

Amy stood in the middle of the office and stared at

the box of receipts. "You haven't done any bookkeeping this year?"

Mac shook his head. "No big deal, it's only the end of February."

"That's easy for you to say." She glanced at the pile of check stubs and moaned. "I guess you haven't done your bank reconciliations, either."

"Nope. Oh, and nobody's been paid in a month. I missed the payroll two weeks ago and it's due again today. I've been giving everybody cash to tide them over."

"Cash? From your personal account?"

He nodded.

She moved behind the desk and slumped into the chair. What was she supposed to do now? Taking over an existing accounting system would have been difficult enough, but starting from scratch—could she do it?

Apparently Mac read her mind. "It's not too late to back out, princess. You can go back to being a silent partner."

She looked up at him. Dark eyes flashed a message she was too inexperienced to read. Did he really not want her here or was he giving her an out? A third possibility flashed across her consciousness. Perhaps he was as nervous about the arrangement as she was. She dismissed the thought as soon as it occurred to her. What on earth would he have to be nervous about?

"I'm here for the duration," she said, stacking the papers on the desk into neat piles. "You can't scare me off. Did you at least keep track of the amount of cash you gave everyone?"

"Of course. Do you think I'm completely irresponsible?"

He pulled a crumpled piece of notebook paper from his back pocket and passed it to her. She smoothed out the sheet and stared at the list of names and amounts. Her heart sank as she realized he'd handed out odd, unrelated sums of cash. "Why on earth did you give Bob thirty-seven dollars and fifty-two cents?"

"It's all I had on me. I'd left my bank card at home and he had a date for lunch. Don't sweat the small stuff. I'm sure with your financial background, it'll be a snap." He sat on the corner of her desk and winked.

"I know you're waiting for me to fall on my face, so don't try to charm me, Napoleon Christopher Spirno."

He winced. "Don't call me that name. You know I hate it."

Amy turned her back on him and flipped on the computer. "Just get out and leave me alone. It's going to take days to get this paperwork in order. Why did you let things get into such a mess?"

"Avoiding what I don't want to do has always been a problem."

She looked over her shoulder. Mac stood directly behind her, his face devoid of expression. He was telling her something important, but she wasn't sure what it was. "What does that mean?"

He shrugged. "I'm the black sheep of the family, Amy. In your eyes that makes me some sort of hero, but the reality is I'm just the guy who refuses to follow the rules. I'm not safe in polite society. You'd do best to steer clear of the likes of me."

Before she could form an appropriate answer, he'd left the office.

Amy sighed. Cryptic messages before lunch, never a

good sign. She turned to the computer and prepared to meet her Waterloo.

The menu on the screen looked easy enough. After pressing the key to bring up the payroll program, she began to search for the instruction booklet.

Three hours later, Amy tossed her reading glasses on the desk and stared out the window. Was death by drowning such a bad way to go?

"Please," she begged the flashing screen. "I have no one else to turn to." The machine was silent.

She'd entered the appropriate information to produce the bi-weekly paychecks, updated the tax and vacation information, and printed out the final wages for the eloped manager and friend. But she didn't have a clue as to how to handle the cash Mac had paid out himself.

I can do this, she told herself. But the statement lacked conviction. Was her mother right? Was she incapable of making it on her own?

"Damn it, no!" Amy sprang to her feet and began to pace the crowded office. "I said I was going to be a partner and I'm going to be one. I refuse to be scared off by a computer and a pile of papers." She pulled a can of soda out of the little refrigerator and took a long drink. "If I can't retreat, I'll just have to advance."

She returned to her desk and thought about pouring her drink on the keyboard. She could always say it was an accident and . . .

Her brain ground to a halt and began backtracking. It couldn't be that easy . . . but it was! A grin spread across her face, the excitement of her discovery sending a tingly feeling of euphoria all the way to her toes.

"I'm right," she told the computer. "You know it and I know it. And you thought you'd win."

After picking up the instruction manual, she turned to the index. There it was, big as life: Advances. She flipped to the appropriate page.

When employees have been given a sum of cash before their regular paycheck . . .

It was after two when Mac returned. In one hand, he carried a blue and green plastic bag bearing the name of a well-known beach front boutique; in the other, a couple of deli sandwiches. He met Bob on the ramp down to the dock.

"Has Amy been out of the office?" he asked.

The young man frowned in concentration. "I don't think so, man. Maybe she and the computer are working things out, ya know? I gotta run. The fish bait truck broke down and I'm gonna pick up the order. Later, man."

"Later."

Mac moved toward the office and pushed open the door. Amy sat hunched over the keyboard. Round horn-rimmed glasses perched on the end of her perky nose and made her look like a studious pixie. Tufts of blonde hair stood out from her head as though she'd spent much of the morning yanking on the strands.

"Don't let me down, baby," she said softly. "I know this is right." She hit a key, then pounded her hands on the table when the printer began to hum. "Yes. I'm great. It's that simple. A superior brain. No question. I . . ."

She looked up and saw him standing in the door way. "Uh, hi. How long have you been here?"

"Not long."

"Oh. I, ah, got the paychecks done," she said, assuming a nonchalant pose as she pulled the glasses from her face and ran her hands through her hair.

The flush staining her smooth cheeks made him want to laugh out loud, but the fearful look in her eyes held him back. She was waiting to be chastised for her behavior.

"Our employees will be happy to hear that," he said. "You did good, Amy."

"Thanks."

Her shy smile made him feel as if he'd just slain a dragon. He dropped his packages on the desk. "I've brought you something."

"I hope it's lunch. I'm starving. Getting this sucker going is hard work."

He pointed to the deli bag, then opened the refrigerator and pulled out a couple of sodas. By the time he'd popped the tops and handed her one, she was already making a sizable dent in one of the sandwiches.

Mac settled on the old vinyl sofa and propped his feet up on a box. His own food sat untouched on his lap. The enjoyment Amy got from her meal was enough to take away his appetite . . . for roast beef on rye, anyway.

Before they'd left the house, she'd replaced her dress with pink shorts and a matching tank top. One strap of her cotton shirt had slipped down one arm, leaving the slender strap of her bra in view. Her skin was the color of clotted cream; winter in Denver wasn't conducive to tanning, hence the second bag.

"If you can tear yourself away from your lunch, I brought you something else."

Her blue eyes glanced up at him, then down at the second package. "Really?" She dropped the sandwich and wiped her hands on a paper napkin. Anticipation lit her face from within. He wondered when was the last time someone had given Amy a spontaneous gift.

She pulled open the sack and took out several bottles. "It's sunscreen. Thanks, Mac."

He shrugged. "I didn't want you to get sunburned. Even walking around the dock can be a problem. You've been away a long time, so make sure you're careful. I even got you some colored zinc oxide for your nose."

Wrinkling the feature in question, she giggled. "People will think Bob and I are *both* from another planet."

"Maybe. But better to look silly than to be in pain, princess."

She opened one of the bottles and stood up. After pouring some of the coconut-scented lotion into her hand, she began smoothing the cream on her arms and the small area of chest visible above the scooped neck of her top. He drew in a deep breath. Raising her foot to the chair, she began to apply the lotion to her legs. He let the breath go. She didn't have the slightest clue as to what her innocent dance was doing to him.

Mac pictured her pale and trembling, like she'd been last night. Only in his mind she was wearing one of those lacy, gossamer things women bought specifically to drive men wild. He'd take her in his arms and rip the thin silk from her milky thighs, then lose them both in an uncharted paradise. The image of her light skin against his tan caused a shudder to tear through him.

"This is lovely. Thanks, Mac." Her voice broke into his fantasy and recalled him to the office. She sniffed the bottle one more time, then put the cap on and stored it in the drawer. "Aren't you going to eat?"

He glanced down at the untouched sandwich. The paper bag hid the bulge in his shorts. "Not just yet, thanks. You've forgotten your nose."

"Here." She opened the tube of zinc oxide and smoothed a pink stripe down the center. "What do you think?"

He grinned. "It's very you."

The phone on the desk rang. Mac motioned for Amy to pick it up.

"Spirno Charter. May I help you?"

The happiness in her face drained away so swiftly he wondered if he had imagined it. Her lips were suddenly drawn together in a tight line and she tugged restlessly at a strand of hair. "Hello to you, too, Mother. Yes, I had every intention of calling."

Great. The wicked witch of the east was making her appearance right on schedule. Damn Lynn for interfering in her daughter's life and damn Amy for letting her. Impatience boiled within him. He wanted to grab the receiver away and tell his stepmother to take a hike. But that would solve nothing.

Amy continued to answer questions, her replies getting shorter and more defensive with each passing minute. The confident woman who had conquered the computer just a few brief minutes ago had disappeared. In her place was a shy, scared, insecure young woman struggling to make her own way.

He wasn't completely happy with the partnership arrangement, but having Amy in the office was less distressing than he'd thought. However, while part of him admired her decision to stand up for what she wanted, part of him wondered if her plans included taking charge of everything . . . including his portion of the business.

His ex-wife had married him simply to insure a partnership in the family's prestigious Miami law firm. It had taken him about three years to figure it out. And when he had, he'd sworn never to buy into another long-term commitment. He liked women, always had, always would, but he didn't trust them. Fortunately for him, most ladies seeking marriage knew his free and easy style didn't lend itself to a house with a white picket fence and all the trimmings. They knew to stay clear of him. Was Amy experienced enough to do the same?

Mac remembered a Christmas nine years before. It had been one of his rare appearances home, when he'd brought his bride to meet the family. Amy had been nineteen and already a beauty. Even then he'd felt drawn to her. Whenever he'd been convinced he had her pegged, she'd come out with an outrageous comment that dazzled and delighted him.

He'd been on his way to speak with his father, when he'd heard Lynn talking in the library. She was complaining about Amy. Would she be able to find a man on her own? Would she take the right job? Lynn considered her oldest daughter brilliant; her middle, stunningly beautiful. But Amy was nothing special. He'd started for the door, ready to break in and defend his favorite stepsister, when a sound had caught his attention. In the far corner of the hall, tucked behind the coat rack, stood Amy. Tears fell unchecked down her cheeks as she listened to her mother list her flaws, one by one. If he interfered, if he defended her, Amy would see him and know that he'd heard the painful litany. Rather than add to her shame, he'd walked away. He hadn't returned home for almost three years.

"Yes, Mother. Next Sunday. I'll be there. Yes, I'll tell Mac as well . . . Give my love to the judge . . . All right, goodbye."

She replaced the receiver and glanced up. "We've been invited to brunch."

He shook his head. "Sorry, I have other plans."

"Oh?" She arched one perfect eyebrow. "And what might they be?"

"I'll tell you when I make them."

"Mac! Be a nice son and visit your father for brunch. It won't kill you."

"You're more generous than I'd be. Don't you ever think about telling your mother to leave you alone?"

She toyed with the paper her sandwich had been wrapped in, first crinkling, then smoothing out the sheet. "Of course, I do. I left Florida to get away from her and the rest of the family. When I decided to take charge of my life, I chose to come back. If I can make it here, with everybody trying to tell me what to do, nothing can ever stop me again. I'm making changes, and one of them includes my relationship with her."

"I admire your courage. I think I'd head for the hills rather than face your mother."

Amy chuckled. "Yeah, right. You've always been the one to go after what you wanted." She motioned to the window. "You've got the business, Mac. What else do you want?"

You. The word came out of nowhere, but he didn't deny its truth. He wanted her. Little Amy. From the first time he'd seen her picture, she'd wormed her way into his life. Now, with a new thread of determination adding steel to her spine, he found her irresistible.

She'd been married. She knew what went on between a man and women. If he were to tell her what he was thinking, would she be shocked? Did she think of him as a business associate, or something more?

Her eyes held his. The color darkened by slow degrees until the blue became indigo and the indigo flared into fire. The voice of reason reminded him that he didn't play his games that close to home. That she was still family and not the type to understand his no-commitment rule. She was the kind of woman a man took on forever. But the hunger was strong.

Her creamy skin cried out for his touch; her sweet lips begged to be tasted and savored. Six months was a long time to spend with someone. Too bad he couldn't let himself take advantage of the opportunity to find out exactly how much Amy had grown up.

"What do I want?" he asked, repeating the question. He stood up and stretched, the movement not quite enough to ease the tension lingering in his body. "I've got everything I need right here."

It was late afternoon when Amy stepped carefully along the walkway. In the four days she'd been working in the office, she'd managed to avoid getting close to the ocean. This time, there hadn't been much choice. Mac was out on a charter trip and there was no one else to deliver Mary's paychecks.

Amy was curious about the woman. She'd met all the other employees—there were fifteen altogether—but Mary had been in the Bahamas with a boatload of fishermen. What sort of a person volunteered for an assignment like that?

As she stepped from the walkway to the dock, Amy took a deep breath and stayed close to the fence. She hated the constant up and down motion of the wooden planks. It was the nineties. Why couldn't someone invent a dock that didn't move with the sea?

Clutching the paychecks in one hand and the railing in the other, she made her way to the last slip. A thirty-five-foot sport-fishing boat was being tied off by a petite blonde woman in bleached denim shorts, a bikini top, and stained tennis shoes.

She looked up as Amy approached. "Hi, I'm Mary." She wiped her palm on the side of her shorts and held out her hand. "You must be Amy. Bob told me all about you."

"I'm afraid to ask what he said."

Mary grinned. Her face was tanned, with the weathered look of someone who'd spent her life in the sun. She appeared to be close to forty. A ponytail hung down from a hole in her blue baseball cap. "He mentioned something about a 'totally cool chick' up in the office."

"That's not too bad, I guess."

"From Bob, that's high praise."

Mary stepped easily from the dock to the back of the boat, then climbed on board. From a cabinet on the side, she removed a half dozen fishing poles and a large tackle box. The gentle bobbing of the boat was enough to make Amy's stomach tighten uncomfortably.

"Want to come on board?" Mary asked. "I've got some great pictures from the trip. We always take instant photographs to capture the moment."

Amy took a step back. "No thanks. Another time. I just brought your paychecks. There's the one from two weeks ago, less the cash Mac's paid you. And here's this week's."

"Great. I've got a mortgage payment to make." The older woman jumped back onto the jetty and took the offered checks, then tucked them in her front pocket. Pulling out the coiled hose by the hook-up box, she turned on the water.

"How long have you worked here?" Amy asked.

Mary aimed the spray at the deck and began washing down the boat's flooring. "I got a part-time job while I was in high school and I've been here ever since." She sighed. "Seems like just yesterday Nappy was bellowing out orders and Mac was constantly underfoot. Oh, I almost forgot." She shut off the water and walked over to an ice chest. Inside was a paper-wrapped package. "Could you take this home? It's marlin, for Mac."

Amy tucked her hands behind her back. "Why would he want it?"

"It's fresh. Don't you eat fish?"

"Not when it has eyes and a tail still attached."

Mary laughed. "I already took care of that. Here."

She shoved the parcel forward until Amy had no choice but to accept it. "You gutted a fish? On purpose?"

"It's part of my job."

"I think I'll stick to the office."

Mary shook her head. "Then you'd better tell Mac not to troll on the trip tomorrow."

"What trip?"

"Didn't he tell you?"

Amy swallowed against the tightness in her throat. "Obviously not. What trip?"

"The company has a forty-foot sailboat that we charter to sail up and down the Keys. We just got a cancellation for this weekend, which isn't a problem, but the group picking it up Saturday is expecting to go from Miami to Key West, not the other way around. So, someone has to bring the ship up here."

"Can't you just tow it or something?"

"No. You and Mac are sailing it up."

"I don't think so." Amy backed up two more feet, until her back was firmly pressed against the railing. "I don't like the water. Besides, Mac's the one in charge of the boats, not me. You must have misunderstood."

Mary shrugged as if to say it wasn't her problem. Amy said good-bye and hurried back to the office. She had to get home and fast. There was absolutely no way she was getting on a boat. She'd rather die. She'd rather go live with her mother.

By the time she heard Mac's motorcycle in the driveway, Amy had already paced herself into a semi-panic and her temper wasn't far behind.

"What were you thinking of?" she asked as he walked in the door.

"Excuse me?"

Taking a deep breath to steady her voice and bring it down a couple of octaves, she tried again. "I spoke with Mary a little while ago and she tells me that you expect me to sail a boat." Fear and anxiety added another layer to the subtle attraction she always felt when Mac was in the room.

He placed his helmet on the table beside the door and stretched. "Yeah, so?"

"Yeah, so? Yeah, *so*?" The last syllable was a screech.

Mac glanced at her and frowned. "Do you have a problem with that?"

Throwing her hands up in the air, she stomped back into the living room. "Yes, I do. First, I don't like the ocean. I don't like being in it, or on it, or having any portion of my body touching it. Second, you said that the office was my responsibility and the boats were yours. I thought we agreed there'd be no crossing the line. And third, I don't like you making a decision that involves me without checking with me beforehand."

He pulled off his T-shirt and rubbed it against the back of his neck. After balling the cloth up in his fist, he glanced at her. "Are you done?"

She stared at his bare chest. Dark hair swirled and curled down his stomach. The skin was tanned and smooth, sliding sensuously over the ropes of muscles as he moved. Wanting—greater than propriety, almost greater than her fear of him—urged her feet forward. She took a single step and stopped. The tips of her fingers tingled in anticipation . . . anticipation that would never be assuaged. It had only been four days and she was already on the verge of losing control. How would she manage six whole months?

Mac crossed the room and touched his free hand to her chin. The touch burned as much as it excited; she listened to her heart thundering in her ears.

Slowly she raised her eyes—past the flat tightness of his stomach, past the broad expanse of his upper chest, past the wide masculine shoulders. Her gaze lingered on his mouth and she wondered what his lips would feel like if he ever stopped thinking of her as "Little Amy." Did he kiss hard and hot, pushing a woman toward her passionate response; or was he slower, building a fire that threatened to consume them both in a blazing explosion?

"Amy?"

She swallowed. "Huh?"

"Amy, are you listening to me?"

"What? Oh." She tore her attention away from his mouth and glanced up at his eyes. "Were you saying something?"

"I was saying . . ." He sighed with tempered exasperation. ". . . that I didn't have any choice about the boat. The trip up from the Keys is over twenty-four hours. All the staff is booked out for charter trips, and the international rules of the road require that someone be on watch at all times. The route we take crosses several shipping channels."

"But I don't know the first thing about sailing."

"You don't need to. I'll do all the work. I only need a warm body."

She fulfilled that requirement, especially with him walking around half-naked. "I don't think this . . ."

He grinned. "You're management now, kiddo. You've got to take the bad assignments along with the glory."

She tried to ignore the sensation of his hand cupping her jaw, of his fingers rubbing oh-so sweetly against her cheek. "Couldn't I practice on the glory first and deal with the bad assignments later?"

"Coward," he teased.

"You bet." She saluted smartly, then stepped back

and moved into the kitchen. "I admit it freely. The ocean and I do not get along."

Mac followed and poured himself a glass of water and took a long drink. "Come on, it'll be fun. The weather's going to be perfect. Just a light breeze. Think of it as being in a big bathtub."

"I prefer the shower, thank you."

"But the ship is the *Amata*." He walked over to the table and put down his glass. After indicating she take the opposite seat, he grabbed a chair, turned it so it was facing away from the table, and sat down. His forearms rested along the runged back.

"So?" she asked.

"The *Amata* was one of Nappy's favorite ships. I guess you know the name is a derivation of Amy."

"I . . . No. I didn't know that."

"Even if I buy you out, the *Amata* is yours forever. Don't you remember that from the will?"

"I guess."

He stared at the table. She suspected it was a ploy to keep her from seeing his self-satisfied grin. "It's only about thirty hours. It'll be fun. Come on, we'll have a chance to get to know each other."

Sure, she thought. He probably expected her to bring a doll to play with, or maybe a teen magazine. There was only one way she wanted to get to know Mac Spirno, but that wasn't in the cards. Any lingering feelings had to be left over from her school-girl crush. There was no way she was ready to get involved with a man. After twenty-eight years of other people running her life, she suspected her judgment of the opposite sex was poor. Besides, she'd thought Ted was a normal guy and look what had happened there.

Amy hunched lower in her chair and buried her chin in her chest. She didn't want to go on this trip, but there didn't seem to be any way out of it. She couldn't very well announce that she was overcome with lust and didn't trust herself in the small confines of a sailboat. She was an adult. She could control her baser instincts. Who knows, there might even be a miracle. She might discover that she actually liked sailing.

"If I refuse?" she asked.

"I'll have to hire a crew to bring her up. We can't afford that. Or we can cancel the charter."

"Let me guess. We can't afford that either?"

"Right."

Great. If things were this complicated after four days, how would she get through the first month? "All I have to do is sit there?"

"Promise." He made an X on his chest and raised his palm. "Scout's honor."

"And you agree to this with the understanding that I don't know a thing about boats?"

He nodded.

She sighed. The expression "caught between the devil and the deep blue sea" had never seemed so appropriate. "Just don't make me gut fish," she said finally.

"I won't even make you *eat* fish." Mac leaned over and ruffled her hair. "This'll be great. Leave everything to me. All you have to bring is a change of clothes. We'll leave at six in the morning and drive down to Key West to pick up the boat."

Amy zipped up her overnight case and glanced out the window. It was still dark outside. If the sun wasn't up at five-forty, why was she? She fumed as she remembered the way Mac had ruffled her hair the previous night. Geez, he was treating her like the family pet. Well, she'd show him. They had thirty hours together. She was going to be adult and sophisticated, bowl him over with her wit and charm.

"Stupid man," she mumbled as she slipped on her windbreaker. "Still thinks I'm a child. I'll show him."

But as she walked down the hall, her new-found courage failed. The sound of Mac's cheerful whistling made her want to crawl back in bed and pull the blankets up around her ears. Why had she agreed to this insanity?

She stepped into the living room. The answer was simple. She had something to prove and ocean or no ocean, she was going to do it.

Mac quickly filled the ice chest. They'd barbecue steaks tonight, he thought. There was a hibachi on board. He grinned as he remembered Amy's claim of not wanting to fish. She was in for a surprise. He planned to make this the best thirty hours of her life.

His fingers clenched as he remembered the feel of her face cupped in his palm. All satin smooth and heady perfume, she could turn any man's head. The familiar warning that she was strictly business had barely registered when he looked up and saw a bottle of champagne in the back of the refrigerator. He couldn't. He shouldn't. What about his rules?

Why the hell not? Wasn't everyone always telling him that he lived to break the rules? A man and woman, alone at sea. Who knew what could happen?

FOUR

By the time the sun was several degrees above the horizon, they were speeding south on the highway. Amy had turned down Mac's invitation to breakfast. The closer they got to the boat, the less her stomach could handle the thought of food. Even now, knots of tension were pressing uncomfortably against the waistband of her shorts. In all the rush to get ready, she hadn't had time to go to the drugstore and buy motion sickness medicine. Maybe if she offered a quick prayer to the sea god, she'd get through the trip with her insides intact.

As they left the mainland of Florida and headed out over a bridge, Amy began giving herself a stern lecture. This was going to be okay, she reminded the part of her that begged to turn the car around. Thousands of people went sailing and survived. What was the worst that could happen?

But picturing herself as the day's main course for a

great white shark didn't soothe her nerves. She thought about asking Mac if there were any sharks in the water, but decided ignorance was the better part of valor . . . especially since retreat was out of the question.

Taking a deep breath, she tried to settle back in the seat. The drive south would be about three hours. There was no point in becoming hysterical before they arrived at the marina. She should save her strength for the actual boating itself.

The car ran quietly; the powerful engine under the long sleek hood purred like a contented tiger. She'd been surprised when Mac had backed the red sports car out of the garage. He'd always seemed to be such a part of his motorcycle, it had been startling to see him with a regular automobile. With a grin designed to melt the heart of the coldest ice maiden, he'd explained that most women didn't like their dates showing up with a bike and an extra crash helmet. Privately, Amy decided the ladies in question were fools.

The low, leather seat was comfortable, she thought as she shifted around. The scent of the leather mingled with her own perfume and Mac's aftershave. Too bad she couldn't bottle the combination and sell it. She could call it "Pheromone Phancy," and make her fortune. Heaven knows it was working on her. Even without her morning coffee, the smells were making her mouth water . . . but not for breakfast. The hunger went much deeper. It was the hunger for a man; not just any man, but specifically the one only inches to her left.

Slowly, she turned to glance at him. As always, his handsome, tanned features jump started her heart. She'd expected him to be casual on the trip, but he'd shaved that morning. Was it for her? Even as the question flitted through her mind, she pushed it away. Of course not, she answered herself. That would imply that he was interested in some sort of a relationship. She was just his business partner, the one who got in the way and tormented his life. She sighed.

"That sounded serious." Mac's voice was still scratchy with the lingering effects of sleep. It made her wonder how he'd sound in the middle of the night . . . when he leaned over to take her in his arms and love her until the dawn.

Shaking her head, she straightened up in the seat. "I was just thinking about things."

"Like?"

"Oh, I don't know. That you must think I'm a pain in the butt, always getting in your way."

He turned and gave her a quick glance. "Bite your tongue. I like you, Amy. I always have. I still have that picture you painted for me."

"Really?" Even to her own ears, her voice was filled with adoring worship. One year, she'd painted a seascape for him. It had been the view from one of her boarding schools; tall dunes and waves of long grass giving way to the violent sea just before a storm. She preferred pictures of flowers or people, but Mac always loved the ocean.

Calm down, she told herself. It didn't mean a thing. But that didn't stop the warm glow from settling around her heart. "It wasn't very good."

"I loved it. Still do. It's hanging in my bedroom."

"Oh." So the picture saw what she had only dreamed of. "I've always felt badly that you didn't tell us about Jenny. I had the picture for you, but never got her anything for a gift.''

Nine years ago, Mac had shown up for Christmas. His unannounced visit had thrown everyone into a tailspin, especially when he had brought his new bride. Even now, Amy could remember her feelings of envy and resentment when she'd seen the dark-haired beauty. Jenny was tiny and smart and beautiful, all the things Amy had longed to be.

Mac laughed. ''I don't think we got a divorce because you didn't buy her a present.''

''I know, but . . .'' She looked out the window. The bridge swept low, close to the sparkling ocean. On the horizon, a sail snapped in the gentle breeze. Soon that would be them. Her stomach knotted in protest. ''I remember the two of you sitting in the study with your dad talking about the law. I admired her for being so knowledgeable. I was still trying to decide on my major, and she was already married and working for the firm.''

He reached out and patted Amy's bare knee. At the contact, the nerves in her leg raced up and down, colliding with each other and sending sparks in all directions.

''You were still a kid,'' he said. ''What, eighteen?''

''Nineteen.''

''See? Jenny was twenty-six. But I don't think that would have made a difference. She was born old.''

''You sound as if you disapproved of that.''

Lean fingers moved impatiently on the steering wheel. ''She knew what she wanted and she went after it. She wanted a partnership in a prestigious law firm. I was her ticket in.''

Amy felt her mouth drop open. "Are you saying she married you because your father was the senior partner in the practice and she thought it would help her career?"

"You sound shocked."

"I . . . I am. I can't imagine such a thing. That's awful. Are you sure?"

"How did you get to be so grown-up and stay so innocent? Yeah, I'm sure. As soon as we were married, she started bugging me to go back to law school. It didn't matter to her that I loved the dock and the boats. She was only interested in her career." His jaw tightened as he down shifted to pass a slow truck. "When I caught on to what she was doing, I confronted her. She didn't deny what she'd done. We stayed together for a couple of years after that, but it wasn't the same. Even when she said she really cared about me, I couldn't forget the real reason she'd wanted to get married." He spoke matter-of-factly, but she could hear the pain lingering in the words.

"That must have hurt you very much," Amy whispered.

"It taught me two very important lessons. The first is, women will take whatever they want, regardless of who it belongs to. The second, don't get involved."

"What do you mean?"

"Just what I said. I'm not interested in commitments of any kind."

She started to argue with him, but then was silent. In her mind's eye, she saw the stunning Jenny seated before the fire. Her brown eyes had sparkled with wit and intelligence. Was it possible that had been a mask for a greedy nature?

Poor Mac. She looked at him cautiously, then turned away. No wonder he hadn't remarried. If he thought that all women were only interested in what they could get from him, then . . .

Oh no. She nibbled on her bottom lip and stared out the window. Maybe he thought *she* was out to get what she could from him. After what Jenny had done, she couldn't blame him for thinking she was after more than just her half of Spirno Charter. Should she tell him she had no interest in more than her share? He wouldn't believe her if she tried. Better to wait and show him she only wanted to be a partner, not a sole owner.

"What about you, princess?" he asked. "How come you've never remarried?"

"Me? I don't have room for a man in my life." She chuckled to herself. "I'm only interested in keeping my head above water." She glanced out the window and instantly regretted her analogy. "What I mean is, my intent is to take charge of my life. In my experience, men like women to defer to them."

"We're not all that bad, are we?"

"I doubt it, but how would I know? Most of the guys I dated were sons of my mother's friends. I wouldn't know a decent man if I tripped over him."

Mac pointed to the diner up ahead. "Last call for breakfast."

"I'll pass. You can stop if you want. I don't mind watching you eat."

"I'm fine. You're the rookie at this. Just trying to be a nice guy."

As soon as Mac spoke, he wanted to call the words back. By echoing what she had said a minute before, he couldn't help but wonder if Amy thought of *him* as a decent guy. He wasn't, he thought as he remembered the champagne tucked in the ice chest. At least not decent in the way she meant.

Amy needed someone who would always be there for her. Someone responsible and capable of putting her needs first. He was a selfish bastard, as his father had pointed out on more than one occasion. He went where he wanted, when he wanted, and to hell with the rest of the world. All his life, he'd fought against the rules. Amy needed the rules, they were her anchor.

She was home port, seeking the familiar, the constant, knowing what would be today and in the future. He was the sea, changing, shifting moods, moving with the tide and wind. Coexistence was possible, union unlikely. As long as they both understood that, they'd get along fine.

He opened the sun roof and rolled down the windows. "Smell that fresh air. You can almost taste the sea."

"Uh-huh." Amy hunched down in her seat. "It's great. When did you first start working at the dock?"

"Nappy brought me down before I could walk." He smiled at the memory. "By the time I was eight, I had my own sailboat and was making trouble all over the marina."

"Didn't you ever want to do anything else?"

He shook his head. "I've always loved the sea. I like the openness. No matter how many times you go out, it's always different and challenging. I remember once I got caught in a storm. The wind was fierce, screaming in my ears like a banshee. The boat rocked up and down endlessly. Waves crashed over the deck and I thought . . ."

"Mac?" Amy put her hand on his arm. "Could we change the subject?"

"Sure." He glanced at her face. All the color had drained away, leaving behind a grayish-green tinge. "What's wrong?"

"Nothing, I just don't want to talk about your near-death experience just before I set foot on a sailboat."

"Sorry. Tell me about the last time you went out."

She took a deep breath. The green faded, leaving her pale but less sickly looking. "Out where?"

"On the ocean."

"You mean on a boat?"

He nodded.

"Never."

He couldn't have heard her correctly. "What?"

"I've never been sailing before."

"Why didn't you say something?"

She twisted to look at him. "I told you I couldn't sail."

"I know, but I assumed you'd been on a boat before."

"Why? What difference would it have made? You told me I had to go. I didn't think my lack of experience would matter."

"Of course, it would matter. You should start out with a short afternoon on a clear, smooth day. Not an overnight trip. What if you get seasick?"

"Believe me, I've thought of that." A flicker of humor lit her blue eyes. "That's why I'm not keen on eating. Anyway, you told me the weather would be clear. Are you trying to say we may have a storm?"

"No. It will be flat and calm, and you'll be fine."
He brushed his fingers against her cheek. "I just wish
you'd told me before we left."

"I didn't want to let you down," she murmured.

Typical, Spirno. Amy hadn't even been working with
him for a week and he'd already intimidated her into
keeping quiet about her fears. His father was right, he
was selfish and self-serving.

He gave her face a last, brief caress, then put his
hand back on the gearshift. They were almost at the
boat. No matter how difficult, he'd do everything in
his power to make Amy's first sail pleasant and un-
eventful. No tacking against a stiff breeze, no sudden
maneuvers. It would be as easy as riding a merry-go-
round.

"Anything else I should know?" he asked playfully.
"Are you claustrophobic?"

She smiled tightly. "Not that I know of."

Amy picked up her overnight bag and hesitated by
the car. She could see the boat tied up at the slip. It
was all white with a thin blue line of trim. The silver
mast reached high up toward the sky. Even in the quiet
of the marina, the ship moved up and down with the
waves.

There was no way she was getting on board, Amy
thought as Mac continued to unload supplies from the
car. She'd have to tell him the truth: She was terrified
of the water and couldn't possibly sail with him.

He slammed the trunk shut. "All ready?"

"Ah, what do you do about your car?" she asked
desperately. Maybe he'd forgotten they'd have to leave

it in the parking lot. Maybe she could drive it back and . . .

He grinned. "Bob's off tomorrow. He's going fishing with some of his buddies. They'll drop him off here and he'll drive it back. The deal works for both of us. I trust him with the car, and he gets to take a new girlfriend out in it."

"Oh." How convenient, she thought grimly. Escape route one, down; on to plan number two. She looked at the tiny craft. "Are you sure there's room for both of us on board? I wouldn't want to get in your way."

He picked up the ice chest and started down the ramp. "The *Amata* is over forty feet long and sleeps six. I don't think we'll be cramped for space."

She followed him, clutching the railing with one hand, her overnight bag with the other. Obviously, they had different ideas about being confined. Even close up, the craft didn't look that long.

"Besides," Mac said, glancing back at her. "I need a crew member to comply with maritime regulations."

"Oh. Yeah. I forgot."

It was now or never, she thought. The urge to run was strong. No, she told herself. She'd made the decision to take charge of her life. She was the one who'd wanted to claim her half of the business. Mac was right—she had to take the good with the bad. Backing out now would be cowardly and irresponsible.

"She's a beauty, isn't she?" Mac set his load on the dock and stepped into the cockpit. After pulling a key out of his pocket, he unlocked the hatch and folded back the door. "Nappy bought her new, about four years ago. There's virtually no teak outside, which cuts down on the varnishing. I like the older boats better, but she's still got style. Don't you, baby?" He patted the steering wheel lovingly, then held out his hand to Amy. "Come on board."

Taking a deep breath, she moved up the two steps beside the boat, then awkwardly swung her foot to the *Amata*'s deck. The dock was moving, as was the ship, but for some reason known ònly to God and physicists, they weren't moving together. Caught between going forward and falling back, Amy froze in mid-stride.

Mac grabbed her by the waist and set her on the deck. "Look around. I'm going back for the rest of my gear." With one fluid motion, he jumped off and started along the dock.

"Wait! You can't . . ." He moved up the ramp toward the parking lot. ". . . leave me here alone," she finished quietly.

The boat shifted restlessly with the current. Amy bent her knees slightly to compensate. Immediately, her sense of balance returned. That's not so bad, she thought. Maybe she'd survive after all.

Walking cautiously, keeping one hand against the steering wheel, then the hatch, she inched her way toward the cabin. If she sat down below, where she couldn't see the water, she might feel better.

There were three shallow steps, then an open area. While not spacious by any stretch of the imagination, the cabin wasn't as cramped as she had expected. To her left was a U-shaped bench with a table. Custom-made cushions in a soothing rainbow of pastels set off the glowing teak that accented the living area.

On the right was the kitchen . . . no, the galley. In deference to her new job, she'd been boning up on her nautical lingo. Maybe she could impress Mac later. In addition to a sink, there was a four-burner stove, micro-wave, and the smallest refrigerator she'd ever seen. Guess they drank their sodas at room temperature.

Up ahead was a hallway with two closed doors on either side. A quick investigation showed a closet and a tiny bathroom. At the very front of the boat rested a wide mattress, tucked under the vee of the bow. Cup-boards, shelves with bars in front to keep the contents from spilling, and drawers filled every inch of wall space. Nothing was left to chance. Even the TV in the corner of the salon was bolted down. Maybe it was supposed to make her feel secure, but it didn't.

She remembered another hatch behind the cockpit. It was probably the second cabin. Mac had said something about a queen-sized bed and two bathrooms on board. She stowed her bag in the closet and grimaced. This boat slept six people? No way.

I'm strong, she recited silently, as she walked back to the hatch. *I can do this. There's nothing to be afraid of. I chose to be here.*

A thump on the deck above her head signaled Mac's return. He stuck his head into the hatchway. "What do you think?"

His dark eyes flashed with excitement and expecta-tion. She could no more tell him the truth than she could spank a puppy. "It's really great," she said, tucking her hands in her back pockets. "I can't wait to get going."

"Underway," he corrected.

"Oh, thanks." She smiled with what she hoped was sincerity and grabbed the ice chest he was lowering. "I'll put the groceries away while you do your . . . underway stuff."

His grin caught her like a two-fisted blow to the ribs. "This is going to be fun, princess. You wait and see."

Fun? Right. If the world chose this moment to come to an end, she'd wouldn't complain. She'd throw a party!

Mac started the engine and motioned for Amy to cast off. She glanced over her shoulder, as if she were about to protest, then tossed the line back onto the dock. Her progress from the bow back to the cockpit was slow and unsteady; one hand clutched the lifeline, the other the grab rail. Her athletic shoes squeaked on the deck.

He had a good feeling about the trip. She was a little nervous, but that was understandable. He frowned. If only she'd told him she hadn't sailed before. Not that he'd expected an experienced crew member, but there was a big difference between a weekend sailor and a novice.

He grinned. Actually, it might not be all bad. A full moon . . . a sky full of stars . . . what woman could resist? He glanced at his watch. Night was a long way off—too long for him.

"I have a present for you," he said when she joined him on the bench.

"Oh?" Her blue eyes lacked the sparkle he was used to.

"Is something wrong?"

"No. Why do you ask?"

"You have the oddest expression on your face. How do you feel?"

She patted her stomach. "Not too bad, considering. Everything's staying where it's supposed to. What's the present?"

"In a minute. Let's get underway. Then we can talk." He eased the motor into reverse and began the slow process of backing the boat out of the slip.

When they'd cleared the finger of the dock, he increased the power and they moved toward the main channel and the open sea. Up ahead a single cloud chased across a clear blue sky. The sun was warm and bright. He inhaled the clean smell of the air while Amy continued to sit patiently next to him.

"A man with a parrot on his shoulder walked into a bar," she murmured softly.

"What are you talking about?"

"Ah, nothing." She smiled brightly. "Just this habit I have. You said something about a present?"

"Lift up that cushion," he said, pointing to the bench across the cockpit. "You'll find a storage compartment underneath."

Amy scooted around the steering wheel and opened the hatch. Inside was a plastic bag filled with deck shoes. She held up a pair. "This is it?"

He laughed at her disgusted tone. "Yes. They're better on the boat than tennis shoes. Look at the soles."

She turned one over. "The bottom is rubber. It's cut. Are these used?"

"No, princess. The slits allow the shoes to grip the deck more firmly when you're walking around."

She glanced at the open ocean and shuddered. "I didn't plan on doing my aerobic workout today. What about the net part on top?"

"If water splashes on board, it just drains out the bottom of the shoes. Pretty clever, huh?"

The pair fell from her hands and bounced on the

deck. "W—water? Why would there be water on the boat?"

Mac stepped forward and took her hands in his. "It's okay. Sometimes a wave splashes over the bow. There's nothing to worry about."

Her eyes grew wide and the blush on her cheeks faded to gray. "You didn't tell me that. I didn't know that." After pulling free of his grasp, she began tossing the rest of the cushions in the cockpit and throwing open the hatches.

"What are you doing?"

She didn't look up from her task. "I need a life jacket. If water can splash on, then I can splash off." She stood up and clutched his shirt. "Where are they?"

"Amy, calm down. The sea is perfectly flat today." He turned her body until she was facing the ocean. "Not a single whitecap. Nobody's going overboard."

He placed his hands on her shoulders. Slight tremors racked her body; he felt the vibrations down to his toes.

She took a deep breath. "I'm sorry to be so silly. You're right. I'll be fine. It's just . . ."

"Yes?"

"I can't swim."

Mac didn't remember exhaling, but suddenly there wasn't any air in his lungs. "What?"

She began putting the cushions back in place. "I never learned. Nobody at home taught me, and at school I played other sports."

He swore out loud, then slammed his fist against the steering column. "What the hell were you thinking of? You can't swim? Didn't it occur to you I might like to know that piece of information? I *am* responsible for your safety.'' He heard his voice getting louder and drew in a deep breath.

"Safety?" she repeated, spinning to face him. "Right. You're the one who forced me to come with you."

"I did no such thing."

"Oh, please." She planted her hands on her hips. Blue eyes flashed with anger. "That entire song and dance about having to hire another crew was designed to make me feel guilty. Don't yell at me because it worked."

He stepped closer and glared down at her. "I am *not* yelling."

"You are, too." She stared out at the marina. "Look. I'm sorry I didn't tell you I couldn't swim. But that doesn't change anything. I'm here, aren't I? Can't we just make the best of it?"

"That's easy for you to say. But I'm the one who has to worry about you doing something stupid like falling overboard."

"You're really angry, aren't you?"

"Yes."

"Oh." She glanced down at her feet. "I know I should have told you. It's just . . . I knew you'd be upset."

"Damn right I'm upset." He started to turn the boat around.

"What are you doing?"

"Taking you back."

"But I thought you needed me to come with you?"

"I'll make other arrangements."

"Mac, please." She raised her eyes to the sky. "Why am I begging to stay on board? I don't want to be here . . . but I need to be here. Look. I'll be the perfect passenger. I'll stay out of your way. I'll do everything you tell me."

He hated it when she stared up at him with such childlike trust. He hated it more when the look made him feel like a jerk. There was every reason for him to be irritated. Keeping her on board would be crazy. His gaze dropped to her heaving chest. Maybe crazy was the wrong word.

As quickly as it had flared, the anger died and his good humor returned. "All right. You can stay, but you *will* follow orders without question. Do you understand?"

"Aye, aye, captain." She gave him a mock salute.

"Good. The first order of business is to get you protected."

The movement of the boat changed subtly and Mac knew they'd left the marina for open sea. He pulled open a compartment tucked under the deck and removed one of the life jackets.

"Number one quality, triple inspected," he said as he pulled it over her head. "Lightweight, guaranteed to float for forty days and thirty-nine nights."

"Very funny."

He straightened the straps across her back and brought them around to meet the clip in front. His hands, normally so confident in their movements, stumbled when his knuckles brushed the underside of her breast. The brief contact was electric. Not by a whisper did she acknowledge whether or not she'd noticed, but he felt it. His blood bubbled hotter, urging him to touch the tender flesh again. Tonight, he thought.

"I'll put up the sails, princess. Then you can fix some brunch."

She adjusted the thick device around her neck. "You expect me to cook in that tiny . . ." He raised one eyebrow. "Of course, Mac. I'd be delighted. Perhaps later I can shine your shoes."

Mac checked the chart and verified they were on the correct heading. The sound of Amy working below in the galley, the off-key humming punctuated by an occasional curse, made him grin. He knew she'd like sailing once she got the hang of it.

The boat heeled slightly to starboard, the wind snapped in the sails.

"Is there any way to make this vessel sail level?" she asked.

"Sorry, no. We go with the wind."

"Figures," she said, holding onto the plates while she walked up the stairs. Leaning against the open hatch, she grinned. "I don't cook well at an angle. Hope you weren't expecting anything fancy."

He took the food and waited until she came back with the coffee. "Looks great."

She'd made omelettes with lots of cheese and vegetables. There was toast and even hash browns. Amy braced one foot on the steering wheel and dug in with enthusiasm. "I'd always heard that boating gave people an appetite, but I'd never believed it before. This is delicious." The coffee mugs swung from braces on either side of the steering column.

He glanced at her. The orange of the life vest clashed with the red of her T-shirt. Her windblown hair stuck up in uneven tufts. She was completely adorable.

The sailboat continued to head northeast. The sea would pick up a little as they moved up the Keys. He made a note to make sure to keep the sails loose enough to make the trip slow and easy.

"I was getting a little concerned," she said between bites. "My stomach felt funny for a while, but I think it was just rumbling because I was so hungry."

A sliver of apprehension trickled down Mac's spine. "Amy, maybe you should go easy on your meal."

"Why?" The happy expression on her face faded.

"I . . . No reason. You're right. I'm sure you were starving. After all, you skipped breakfast." When her smile returned and she continued eating, he told himself there was no reason for Amy to get seasick. A lot of people didn't. If she was going to react to the motion, it would have happened by now.

After brunch, he left her at the helm and took the plates down to the galley to wash them off. The wind began to pick up, moving the craft more swiftly through the sea. Waves grew larger, the up and down motion more pronounced.

He stepped behind her at the wheel and pointed to the compass. "Keep that heading. You need to turn a little. Otherwise, we'll miss Florida and end up in Ireland."

Amy smiled weakly and stepped back. "You do it, Mac. I think I want to sit down."

"Do you feel all right?" he asked, touching her face.

"Not really." The greenish cast was back. Even her lips were pale. "I think eating was a big mistake. I'd better get to the bathroom and . . ."

"No." He cut her off. "Using the head below will make it worse. If you have to throw up, just lean over the side."

"I couldn't do that, I . . ." Her sentence was lost

as she lunged to the left and stuck her head out past the railing.

By the time she had finished, Mac had returned from below. He handed her a damp washcloth and a cup of water. "Rinse your mouth out. You'll feel better."

"Thanks," she said weakly. "Sorry to be such a pain."

"No problem." He sat next to her and brushed the hair out of her eyes. Why did this have to happen now? he wondered. She'd been such a trooper about everything that had happened, she sure as hell didn't deserve to be seasick. "It's my fault anyway. If I hadn't gotten upset with you, you wouldn't have insisted on coming with me. I'm sorry, princess." He felt as low as a garden slug and just as stupid. How could he have been so selfish?

"Mac, that's sweet, but . . . Oh, God."

He waited until the next episode was over, then propped her up against the rear cabin. A light blanket covered her bare legs and a cup of carbonated water was tucked beside her hand. "You'll feel better soon. Once you've been sick, your body will acclimate."

Her eyes fluttered shut. "I hope you're right. I'd hate to feel this awful for the next twenty-four hours."

"You won't," he said softly. "I promise."

By four o'clock, he was regretting his words. Amy had suffered the entire trip. In between bouts of nausea, she was both hungry and thirsty. Whatever she took in, she threw back up.

Mac paced restlessly, as much as the small cockpit would allow. Making a decision, he headed into the cabin.

"Mac, don't leave me," Amy called softly.

He smiled briefly. "I'll be right back. I need to use the radio."

With the help of the marine operator, he was patched through to his office. After a short conversation with Bob and Mary, he turned the equipment off. He'd done what he could. The rest was simply going to take time.

Right, a voice in his head mocked. As though none of this was his fault? He'd bullied her from the start. When he found out she'd never been on a boat *and* couldn't swim, he should have instantly turned around.

Somehow, he'd make it up to her, he promised himself. Even if that meant staying out of her way forever. Slowly, he made his way back to the deck.

"I'm sorry to be such a bother," Amy said from her place in the corner. "I've ruined your whole trip."

"Never." He sat next to her and ran his index finger down her nose. "You didn't know you were going to be so sick. It's too late to turn back, but we'll be heading into a marina in a few minutes. Mary and Bob will meet us there. They'll sail back and we'll drive to the house."

"Oh, Mac." Her blue eyes darkened with tears. "I feel so bad for you. Are you angry?"

Yes, of course he was. But only with himself. He deserved to be keel-hauled, flogged, then buried in salt. Even now, he could hear his father's familiar list of complaints. "You'll be the death of somebody, son. Mark my words. You only think of what you want. You're a selfish bastard and one day you'll pay." At the time, Mac had thought the older Spirno was reacting to the disappointment of learning his only son wouldn't take his place in the family law firm, but now he wondered if the words were more true than he'd been willing to admit. He *was* selfish and unthinking and . . .

He groaned softly as he remembered the bottle of champagne in the bottom of the ice chest. How could he have thought about seducing Amy? He'd always known he wasn't the right kind of man for her; this had proved it in spades. From now on, it was business only. No matter what, he wouldn't touch her or even allow himself to think about making love with her. He'd rather burn in hell than hurt her again.

FIVE

By the time Bob's car pulled into the driveway, Amy was beginning to feel a little like her old self. The violent shifting in her stomach had finally stopped.

Mac shut off the engine and looked at her. "Home, safe and sound."

"Thank goodness. I'm exhausted." She started to open the car door.

"Stay put," he ordered. "You're also weak and dehydrated. I don't want you losing your balance on me."

"I'm not an invalid. I tossed my cookies a couple of times, but I'll survive."

Apparently he didn't bother to listen. Before she could continue with her protest, Mac had walked to her side and scooped her up in his arms.

"Why are you doing this?" she demanded as she held on tight.

"Because I'm big and burly and always get my way," he said.

But she heard the concern behind the words. She might be feeling pale and shaky, but Mac looked as if he'd lived through a war. The lines fanning out from his eyes seemed deeper and more pronounced and the muscles of his back were tight with tension.

Relaxing her arm around his neck, she gave in to his comforting concern. His stride was easy and long, as though he carried women all the time. For all she knew, he made it a habit with his lady friends.

The scent of the sea clung to his clothes and his skin. Now that they were on solid ground, she could appreciate the clean smell. It was fun to be pampered, although she wouldn't want to go through this day again, even for a hundred rides in Mac's arms.

He carried her down the hall and into her bedroom. "Bed or shower?" he asked.

"Shower."

After crossing the floor and stepping into the bathroom, he lowered one arm until her feet touched the floor. "Can you stand?"

"Of course, I can stand. Quit fussing over me. I'm fine."

"Uh-huh. Sell it somewhere else, princess. I'm going to keep an eye on you until I'm convinced you've recovered."

"Oh?"

"Take your clothes off."

She blinked twice, convinced she'd heard incorrectly. "Excuse me?"

"Take your clothes off. Or do you usually bathe fully dressed?"

"I . . . You can't . . . There are . . ."

She sputtered in vain. Without further ado, he turned

on the shower and adjusted the temperature. After placing a fresh towel on the counter, he knelt down to pull off her deck shoes.

"Mac, I really think that . . ." Did he expect her to parade around naked in front of him?

He stood up. "I'm not doing this to seduce you. I just want to make sure you're all right. I'll be outside. Call me if you feel faint." The door slammed shut to punctuate his sentence.

He wasn't trying to seduce her? she repeated quietly. Well, why the hell not?

She turned to look at herself in the mirror. Her skin was red and chapped from the wind. The beginning of a sunburn made her nose puffy. Even her lips were cracked and dry. Not exactly the picture of the all-American beauty, she thought as a giggle escaped. No wonder Mac hadn't blinked when telling her to undress.

So much for bowling him over with womanly charms. She dropped her clothes into a pile, then stepped into the steaming water. Wasn't she supposed to have been witty and charming on the boat ride? As she poured shampoo into her hand and rubbed it into her hair, she reminded herself that there was one bright spot. Things between them couldn't get any worse.

"How do you feel?" Mac asked as he tucked the covers in around her.

Amy rolled her eyes. "Stupid. And hungry."

"Good combination. Dinner's coming right up."

"What are we having."

"Fish."

She swallowed against the lump in her throat. "Please tell me you're kidding."

He sat on the edge of the bed and picked up a tub of cream. "I'm kidding. How about soup and dry toast? You'd better take it easy until your tummy recovers." After touching the ointment to her nose, he paused. "Any other burns?"

She shook her head. "I guess I put sunscreen everywhere else but there."

"Okay."

He started to leave, but she touched his arm. "I'm sorry, Mac."

Dark eyes studied her. Concern and something deeper flickered there. With the window only partially open, the sound of the waves was muted.

His hand brushed her cheek. "Don't. We've been through this before. It was my fault, not yours. We've both learned a good lesson. Dividing the business between us is the best policy. You take care of the land and I'll handle the sea. Now, I'm going to grab a quick shower, then warm up your dinner. Can you wait about twenty minutes?"

She smiled against the gentle pressure on her face. It took every ounce of willpower not to turn her head and touch the tip of her tongue to the pads of his fingers, but she couldn't bear to see him recoil. He'd made it very clear how he felt about her.

She turned away. "I'll survive, but I make no guarantees for anything longer than twenty-five minutes."

Amy pushed away the bowl. "If I eat another bite, I'll burst."

"Do I have to watch that, too?" He ducked the napkin she tossed and set her tray on the floor. "Do you need an aspirin or anything?"

"No. I'm fine. Stop asking me if I need something."

"Excuse me for being concerned."

"Sorry." She leaned back against the pillows. "I'm not usually cranky. I was trying to remember the last time I got this sick."

Mac stretched out on the wicker chair he'd pulled close to the bed and propped his feet up on the corner of the mattress. His dark hair was still damp; it lay across his forehead and curled around the collar of his short-sleeved cotton shirt. "When was that?"

"The morning I got married. Mother was afraid I wouldn't be well enough for the ceremony."

"I thought you looked pale."

She pulled at the oversized T-shirt she was wearing. Afraid to look up, she mumbled her question to the blanket. "Were you *really* at my wedding?"

"I told you I was."

"But I didn't see you."

The room was silent for a moment. "I came in late and stood in the back. When the minister asked you to repeat the vows, you waited so long, everyone began to wonder if you would."

She looked at him. So, he *had* been there. "Why didn't you talk to me? Say hi or something."

She thought he hadn't cared enough to come. How silly that sounded. Mac would never understand the complex role he'd played in her life. At times she'd worshiped him as though he were a rock star, at times she'd needed him to be an older brother, at times she yearned for him with womanly lust. Which emotion was real?

"Your wedding came in the middle of my divorce.

Needless to say, the judge and I weren't exactly on speaking terms. But I did want to see you married.''

Darkness had fallen, reducing their world to the room and its contents. She moved her legs restlessly under the covers. In less than a heartbeat, he was crouched at her side.

He was so very alive. The energy from his body seemed to flow out into the room and press against her. The connection was as real and constant as life itself. She looked at him, wondering how much she should say.

''What is it, Amy?''

She shifted to give him room to sit next to her. The mattress dipped under his weight. One arm stretched across her, bracing his weight on the hand resting next to her hip. The other lay at his side. She longed to ask him to touch her, to hold her until she understood what all her mixed feelings meant, but she was afraid.

A memory, formed more by its echo than any substance, tickled in her mind. She recalled another time, when a strong presence had seemed to hold her close in an endless night of pain. Threaded between the memory of darkness and longing was an impression of comfort.

''Did you visit me at the hospital . . . after I lost the baby?''

He nodded. Taking her hand in his, he held it against his jaw, pressed her fingers against his cheek. ''You were unconscious most of the night. The nurse said you'd be fine, but I wanted to stick around until the fever broke.''

In her mind, she heard half-formed words and partial

phrases. "You told me stories, didn't you? About the sea and growing up."

"Yes."

After only four months of pregnancy, she'd barely begun to show. No one had said why she'd lost the child. Her doctor told her it was simply nature's way of correcting a mistake. There was every reason to believe the next child would be fine. But things between Ted and her had deteriorated to the point that there was no next child.

She remembered begging Mac to tell her why the baby had to die. His expression told her he remembered that as well.

"I wanted to make it right for you, Amy. But all I could do was stay close."

"It made a difference. I always wanted to say thank you, but when I woke up, you were gone. Mother said you'd never visited at all. I've always wondered if it were a dream." She bit her lip.

"Don't, Amy," he said. "Don't look at me as if I can solve all the problems of the world."

"I don't think that."

"Yes—you do."

Her fingers drifted to the back of his neck. Playing with the curling strands of black hair, they pressed against his scalp and neck.

Did she reach upward or did he reach down? She wasn't sure. Yet in the next moment, his arms wrapped around her and held her close.

"Damnit, Amy. Don't let me do this." The half-mumbled growl promised as much as it pleaded. Her hands clutched at his back, urging him on.

For twelve years she'd wondered if she'd imagined

the magic of his kiss. When she'd finally learned what went on between a man and a woman, she'd longed to repeat the experience with Mac. Only this time, there'd be no sudden ending to the embrace; this time, they'd travel to that warm, secret place where only lovers can go.

"I need you, Mac," she whispered, then closed her eyes.

The room was silent; the waves against the shore provided mocking counterpoint to the pounding of her heart. For a second, she was afraid he would pull back, then she felt the feather-light touch of his lips on hers. The contact whispered like the stroke of a shadow. Inside, something tightened painfully, then broke into a thousand pieces.

He lingered, testing the parameters of her mouth, exploring the outline, the center, each millimeter of sensitized skin. It was as if he needed to learn everything before going deeper. Tiny sparks accompanied the exploration. They exploded in midair, then fell, leaving burns of need seeping into her skin.

Her hands drifted down his broad back, stopping only when they reached the edge of his shirt. Slowly, her fingers reversed their course. But this time, under the warm cotton. His skin was hot . . . almost liquid. It rippled and flowed under her touch like thick, molten honey.

As she caressed his sides, his mouth slanted against hers. The gentle mating became a battle. His lips parted and his tongue thrust its way inside. She met him at the entrance; tip to tip, side to side, they stroked, circled, tasted. The unexpected assault carried her to the edge. Her breasts swelled and tingled with aching need.

Wanting poured into her blood and dampened the secret place between her legs.

As his tongue discovered her mouth, his hands slipped from her shoulders down her arms. She tried to move away, to allow him to reach her breasts, but the covers held her trapped. She could only wait—impatiently—for his fingers to end her torment.

Moving her hands to his chest, she crept up through the thick matting of hair. When she reached the hard flat nipples, she flicked her nails gently against the nubs. A low sound was captured in her mouth. He shifted slightly, freeing the covers, then slid one hand to cup her breast.

Even with the barrier of cloth between them, she could feel the movement of his fingers kneading the tender flesh. When his lips dropped to her neck, she arched her head back.

"I knew it would be like this," she whispered. "Oh, Mac, I want so much."

Instead of going forward, he suddenly seemed to be in retreat. The hand fell from her breast and his lips abandoned their exploration of her shoulder.

A violent string of curses filled the room.

She touched his face, trying to keep him close, but he'd already left—in spirit, if not in reality. "What's wrong? What did I say?"

He shook his head and refused to met her eyes. "It's not you, Amy. I'm the one who's wrong. I'm no good for you. I wish it could be different, but—"

"If you apologize for what just happened, I'll never forgive you."

"I wouldn't even begin to try."

He did look at her then. The pain and disgust flaring

in his brown eyes made her catch her breath. He was upset . . . but not with her.

"Mac, tell me."

He stood up and touched her hair. "You still pack quite a punch, kid. And as hard as it's going to be, I'm going to do my damnedest to keep my distance."

When Amy finally gathered the courage to leave her room the next morning, she found that all the dawdling had been in vain. Mac had left hours before. His note on the kitchen counter informed her that he had a lot of work at the dock and she should consider taking the day off if she still felt weak.

Just the sight of his strong handwriting was enough to make her knees knock together, but the reaction came from the memory of their passion, not from her recent bout of seasickness.

"Oh, what you do to me," she murmured softly, crumpling the paper into a tiny ball. "Now what? Do we pretend it never happened? Do we talk about it? Do I seek professional help?"

But instead of a trained psychologist, Amy pictured herself sitting across from a fortune teller. Not exactly the route her mother would approve of, she thought with a grin.

After pouring coffee into a cup, she sat down at the round kitchen table. The easiest thing for both of them would be to forget last night. They had simply reacted to the moment. It didn't mean a thing.

Yet she could recall, in minute detail, the wondrous pressure of his mouth against hers, the way his hands had caressed and excited in equal measure. Some part of her, deep inside, cried out for more from this man.

"Don't be a fool," she said aloud.

There was no room in her life for any man, especially Mac. He'd made it clear he wasn't interested in a long-term relationship and she wasn't the one-night-stand type. Besides, she was trying to get her life together. Until she'd made a success of her half of the business, she'd keep romance on hold. She didn't have the experience, or time, or judgment to know a good man from a bad one. To make matters worse, Mac was the best man she knew. Next to him, no guy stood a chance.

Mac put a clean piece of sandpaper in the block and closed the clamps. The long teak deck stretched endlessly in front of him. Working at his current pace, he should finish the job by this time tomorrow. With any luck, the combination of hard work and fatigue would exorcise the demons from his mind.

"Yo! Bossman! Whatcha up to?" Bob sauntered up the steps and climbed on board the sailboat. "I thought Jack and me were going to re-varnish this baby."

Mac rolled into a sitting position and straightened out his knees. "Just keeping my hand in."

"But you hate varnishing, boss. Why would . . ."

Mac glared at the younger man. "I could stop and let you finish."

Bob raised his hands in a gesture of surrender. "No. I don't mind. It's my day off, anyway."

"I know." He dropped the sanding block onto the deck and stood up. "Sorry to be such a bear. I had a long night."

"Was Amy still sick?"

"No. She's fine, but I don't think she'll be in

today.'' He stretched sideways, easing the aching in his back. ''Thanks for sailing the *Amata* back.''

''No problem. She's a beauty.''

Out in the marina, a thirty-foot sports fisherman cruised by the dock. Several young men called out.

Bob waved in acknowledgment, then backed down the stairs. ''Gotta go. I'll be real careful with your car tonight, boss. See ya in the morning.''

Mac watched his employee jog to the end of the dock, then board the boat. As they took off for the open ocean, he remembered leaving the marina yesterday morning. He'd been convinced that everything was going to work out just the way he'd planned it. Amy would enjoy the trip, they'd enjoy each other.

Instead, she'd had a day of being sick and he'd had a night of torture. Just the memory of tossing and turning in a useless effort to find rest made him grimace.

What the hell had he been thinking of, kissing her like that? Even now, heat flared up, sending liquid need to points south.

He knelt down on the deck and resumed his sanding. The tedious work gave him plenty of time to berate himself. Never again, he swore for the thirtieth time. He had rules! More importantly, Amy wasn't one of his toys; she was a forever kind of woman. It didn't matter how much he suffered in the next six months. He was *never* going to forget himself again.

The sound of a car door broke into his internal tirade. He looked up and saw the lady in question walking toward the office. In the slight breeze, her cotton dress pressed against the curvaceous lines of her body. Her hair gleamed like white gold. All slender arms and long legs, she was a vision . . . truly the princess he'd always claimed she was.

Restless hunger made him attack the wood with renewed fervor. If he couldn't control his desire, he'd use it up with hard work. Looked like the boats were all going to get a fresh coat of varnish, whether they needed it or not.

She was off by sixty-three dollars. Amy glared at the bank statement. The error was too large to ignore, but how was she supposed to find it? After totaling up the checks for a second time, she pounded the desk in frustration. She couldn't go to her supervisor and say there was a mistake. As Mac had pointed out a couple of days before, *she* was management now. When she found a problem, she had to fix it herself.

Digging in the bottom desk drawer, she searched for her accounting textbook. Maybe it had a hint on bank reconciliations. After finding the right chapter, she glanced at the clock and groaned. Two hours. It had taken two hours to even realize there *was* an error. At this rate, she'd catch up with her week's work by the turn of the century.

The book informed her that an error divisible by nine was probably a transposed number. In this case, the difference between the right number and the wrong number should be the sixty-three dollars.

"Who knew?" she asked the room. It would be easy enough to find the mistake now. A quick comparison of the checks themselves with the check register showed that Mac had issued a check for one figure and entered it in the book for another. By the different color inks, she assumed he'd probably forgotten about the payment and later wrote down the amount he thought was close.

"Men!"

Tapping her pencil against the desk, she considered for a moment, then turned to the computer. Apart from Mac and herself, two other employees were allowed to sign checks. Typing quickly, she wrote a memo informing everyone that any blank checks taken from the office had to be signed out. She printed three copies and initialed them.

An hour later, she finished the second bank reconciliation and put the statements away. Now that she had the hang of things, next month's should be a snap.

The day flew by swiftly. Unfamiliar tasks were slowly mastered, and by five she had a warm feeling inside. She could do this job. It would take a while to get good at it, but she was beginning to see the light at the end of the tunnel.

There was still, however, the matter of her memo. Picking up her sunglasses, she grabbed the paper and headed for the door. Mac had been avoiding her all afternoon. From her window, she'd seen him working on one of his boats. He'd glanced over once or twice, yet had never bothered to visit. Was he upset because of last night?

"Stupid question," she answered herself. Of course he was upset and avoiding her. Just like she wanted to avoid him.

There was, however, a business to run. They had no choice but to work together. She could be adult enough to ignore what had happened.

As she neared the dock, her stomach tilted wildly. This time it wasn't at the sight of a sailboat bobbing in the water; it was the man working away in the sunlit afternoon. Sometime in the last hour or so, he'd removed his shirt. Sweat trickled down his chest; the individual drops chased each other through a forest of dark hair. His eyes were shaded by the navy baseball cap he wore; his mouth pulled into a straight line of concentration. He crouched on the far side of the cockpit.

She climbed the two stairs and stepped on board. The boat rocked slightly, then settled down into its regular gentle up and down motion.

"Mac?"

His arm slowed slightly in its task of sanding, then resumed. He didn't look at her. "Yeah?"

"I need to talk to you about something."

He straightened up and wiped his forearm across his face. "If it's about last night, I really don't think there's . . ."

"It's not."

"Oh." He looked confused. "What did you want to talk about then?"

"I wrote a memo. I'd like you to read it and, if you approve, sign it."

"Fine. Leave it there." He pointed to a small table next to the steering wheel.

"No. I want you to read it now. You might want to disagree or something."

He glanced at her then. His eyes, in shadow from the cap, gave nothing away, but a muscle twitched high on his cheek. The fine threads of control were visible in the stiff lines of his neck and bare shoulders. He stepped into the cockpit, six-feet-four-inches of hot, sweaty, predatory male.

She wanted him . . . there, in the boat, for all the world to see. She wanted him with a passion that rose and threatened to drown her in a sea of need. She wanted him to take her again and again until every question had been answered, every possibility explored.

She handed him the memo.

Squinting in the bright afternoon, he quickly scanned the lines, then offered the sheet back. "Seems fine to me."

"You're not exempt."

He grinned and the tension between them released. "Never thought I was. In fact, I'd bet money that something I did gave you this idea in the first place."

"Maybe."

He raised one hand toward her face, then dropped it to his side. "You okay?"

The question wasn't about her health. She wasn't okay. She was confused and hot and the tiniest bit afraid. But he didn't want to hear any of that. "Never better."

A boat zoomed by, stirring up the water. As the sailboat rocked, Amy felt herself lean toward him. Her eyes focused on the hard, straight line of his mouth. His taste still lingered in her memory and she wanted more.

Mac picked up a clean piece of sandpaper and toyed with the rough sheet. "I've still got a lot of work to do."

"Me, too." She stepped out of the boat and onto the dock. "I won't be home for dinner. I've got some errands to run and I thought I'd stop by and visit the family."

"Volunteering to see your mother? You're a brave woman." He smiled before turning back to his work.

Not brave enough, she thought as she walked back to the office. But she was trying. There were over five months left before they re-evaluated the partnership. A lot could happen in that amount of time.

"I've been talking with Marianne. She's opening a new boutique in town and is looking for a manager. What do you think, dear?" Lynn Spirno glided across the living room and perched on the edge of the Louis XVI chair. Her champagne blonde hair was caught in a deceptively casual chignon. Silk whispered as she crossed long slender legs. Her upper body was firm and erect, her back careful not to touch that of the chair.

Amy pulled at her cotton skirt and stared into her sherry. "I have a job, Mom."

Lynn winced at the name. Her other daughters called her by her first name, or mother, but Amy steadfastly refused. Growing up, it had been her only victory.

"But the boat dock. It's so unseemly. The sun is terrible for your skin and the smells . . ." She shuddered delicately. "Surely, you can find something more suitable."

Amy glanced around the room. She'd always hated this house. It was too big . . . too cold. The long, wide rooms echoed with excess space. As a child, the house should have been a wonderful place to grow up. There were countless rooms to run in and hide, but she'd been restricted to the nursery upstairs and the garden.

Her sisters hadn't wanted to play with her, somehow understanding their mother's distaste when Lynn's two-month fling with the club's unsavory tennis pro had produced such a physical reminder. The ink hadn't quite dried on the marriage certificate when the divorce proceedings began. He had redeemed himself by dying in an auto accident shortly after, but then Lynn had found out she was pregnant. Amy never quite overcame the feeling of being somehow less than everyone around her.

"I like my job. Besides, I own half the company. I couldn't leave Mac without warning. We're in the process of changing some of the—"

"I'm sure it's all very interesting, dear, but spare me the details." Lynn smiled slightly, careful not to crease the delicate skin around her eyes. "And Mac is one of the reasons I think you should get out of there. I can't imagine what you were thinking of when you agreed to live in that house with him. I've been telling everyone you have your own apartment, but the truth will come out and then your reputation will be ruined."

Amy laughed. "I wasn't aware I had a reputation to worry about. Mom, where I live is my business. Anyway, Mac is a perfect gentleman. Nothing's going on, not that it's anyone's business what I do."

"But he's so . . ."

Amy set her glass on the antique table and stared at her mother. "Yes? Tell me what he is."

Lynn blinked slowly. "There is no reason to speak to me in that tone, young lady. I'm only concerned with what's best for you."

"Then let me live my life and make my own decisions."

The older woman sighed heavily, as though the burden of her recalcitrant child was too much to bear.

It had been a mistake to come, Amy thought as Lynn

changed the subject. She was still recovering from what had happened at sea and had visited her mother for a little moral support. Not a very clever idea, she told herself. But then the last forty-eight hours hadn't been a testimony to her intelligence. Still, she had sailed and lived to tell the tale. She'd managed to conquer the bank reconciliations and had had her first memo approved. Not bad for a woman who until a few weeks ago had been scared of her own shadow. She raised her sherry in a toast. *To me*, she thought with a private smile. Mac ain't seen the half of it yet.

SIX

"It's too hot outside," Amy complained as she walked inside and slammed the front door shut. "And if you make me go to another meeting like this one, I'll never forgive you."

Mac stuck his head out of the kitchen door. "I can't hear you."

She tossed her briefcase on the long, white cloth-covered sofa, then shrugged out of her suit jacket. The linen had started the day crisp and fresh, but a combination of long hours and an unseasonably warm beginning of April had reduced the expensive garment to a limp pile of wrinkles.

Amy hurried toward her bedroom, shedding clothes as she went. Between the meeting with the insurance agent and the interview for an office assistant, she'd missed lunch. The lingering scent of Mac's cooking made her mouth water.

Five minutes later, she was perched on a stool sipping a tall glass of ice water. "It had to have been eighty today," she said as she held the cool container against her forehead.

"Eighty-five. And they're predicting another hot one tomorrow. I thought we'd eat by the pool."

"Fine. Can I help?"

He looked up from the salad he was tossing. "No. I've got everything under control. I'll throw on the steaks in a bit. Just relax."

She nodded her agreement, then leaned forward and rested her arms on the counter. Mac moved with controlled efficiency. His long fingers worked swiftly. Her gaze took in the regulation T-shirt he often favored after work, then dropped down to the shorts clinging to his slim hips.

The casual attire had ceased to send her into a tailspin every time she saw him, but she certainly appreciated the view of a hard, male body. The implied domestic intimacy was a delicious counterpoint to their strictly platonic relationship.

In the last six weeks, they'd made a sort of peace with each other. At work, she continued to learn and conquer the office, while he controlled the boats. At home, they were pleasant with each other, but restricted their conversations to neutral topics. It was only when they met accidentally—passing in the narrow hall, sleepy-eyed first thing in the morning—that the awareness flared. They'd managed to keep everything under control . . . so far.

How long? she wondered as she moved her glass in random circles on the counter. How much longer could she lie awake at night and remember what Mac's kisses had made her feel? How much longer could she stand his careful courtesies? If everything was kept hidden, she'd never get a chance to find out what she felt.

The problem hadn't changed . . . or disappeared. She still didn't have a point of reference in her life. All the boys she'd met in college had been exactly alike—groomed heirs to the family business. Lawyers, accountants, real estate moguls, they had blurred into an undifferentiated mass. Ted had been picked out and approved by her mother, before Amy had even met him. And in Denver, she'd been too busy trying to put the pieces of her life back together to even think about dating.

So where did that leave her with Mac? He was gentle and patient, humorous and fun . . . in short, almost perfect. She knew how he made her feel, but could she trust the feeling? Was it left over hero worship, simple lust, or something more? And what about him? Was his carefully reserved attitude the natural state of a concerned but distant friend, or did it hide something deeper?

He walked by with the raw steaks. "I'm ready to barbecue. Are you hungry?"

She slid off the stool and followed him to the patio. "Starved."

The round outside table had been covered with a bright yellow cloth and set with silverware.

He dropped the meat onto the hot grill, then glanced at her. "You were looking thoughtful inside. Want to talk about it?"

Later, when she recalled the conversation, she comforted herself with the thought that a momentary lapse had allowed the question to escape. But at the instant she spoke, she wondered if she'd lost her mind. "Have you ever been in love?"

Mac set the tongs on the tray by the grill and took a long drink of beer. Things had been getting too quiet, he thought with a sigh. Trust Amy to stir them up.

"No. Taking a survey?"

The blush staining her cheeks told him that she was as startled by the inquiry as he'd been. "No. I don't think I have been either."

"You were married," he pointed out.

She sat in a chair by the table and put down her glass. "So were you."

"I was seduced by a powerful and evil woman."

Amy laughed. "Please."

"All right. You want a serious explanation?"

She nodded.

"I married Jenny because I was dazzled by her. My father and Nappy had been pressuring me to settle down and she was there. As for loving her?" He checked the steaks, then turned to face Amy. "I was angry when I found out she was trying to control me. I was hurt, but not destroyed. When it was over, I walked away with a new set of rules, but not a broken heart. Doesn't sound like a man who was in love. Since then, I've stayed clear of commitments."

"Because you don't trust women?"

"That, and I'm not good husband material."

Amy leaned forward in her chair and rested her elbows on her thighs. "Tell me about a good husband. What should I look for in a man?"

Anyone but him, he thought, then frowned. The idea of Amy being touched or even spoken to by another guy made his fists clench. Down boy, he told himself.

She might be bright and pretty and fun to be with, but she wasn't for him.

She continued to watch him and wait for an answer.

"Someone strong," he said finally.

"Oh, really? As strong as you?"

He glanced at her, but she was studying the plants in the corner.

"I guess. And someone responsible."

"Mmm."

"I don't know, Amy. Ask your mother."

"No thanks. She's the one who picked out Ted."

Her sweet laughter floated across the patio and settled deep in his chest. The sound made him want to hold her so close that he couldn't tell where his wanting ended and her need began. Instead, he turned over the steaks.

"How was your meeting?"

"Great. Let me get the papers. We can discuss them during dinner."

He watched her walk toward the living room. Her slender hips swayed beneath the shorts. Long legs stretched endlessly to the ground and made him wonder how tightly they'd wrap around him in passion. In the last six weeks he'd taken more cold showers than he wanted to remember. If he didn't change the direction of his thoughts, tonight would be no exception.

"I think the new company is a good idea," she said as she came back. "Their medical coverage is more comprehensive and gives a better value for the dollar." She set her briefcase on the table and unsnapped the catch. After putting her reading glasses on, she held out a large piece of paper. "The exact numbers are on the spreadsheet."

Instead of focusing on what she held, he stared at the books partially hidden below a folder. There was a copy of Chapman's *Piloting* and a couple of others on boating and marinas. He picked up a sailing magazine. "Looks like you've been doing your homework."

She shrugged. "I hate feeling stupid and I've been doing a lot of that since I got here. I know that we agreed to keep our halves of the business separate, but there has to be some sort of overlap. What happens if you get sick or take a vacation? I can't depend on Bob or Mary to make decisions for me."

Her argument sounded logical, he told himself, but that didn't stop the seed of mistrust from sprouting. If she could run the entire company single-handedly, why would she want a partner? It would simply be a matter of time until she got some fancy lawyer to cut him out. For a shot at getting Mac into law school, his father would probably be willing to draw up the documents himself.

He was overreacting, he told himself. Amy wasn't like that. Feeling the tension in his shoulders and back, he forced himself to relax.

She touched his arm. "I want to make you proud of me," she said softly.

Her face was as easy to read as the spreadsheet: the need to please mingled with her sweet but unnecessary concern for him. A tentative smile tugged at her cupid's bow mouth and made him want to protect her against everything in the world, including himself. Of course, he trusted Amy.

"I am proud, kid. You're doing a great job. Let me get the steaks before they burn and you can serve the salad. You have until dessert to convince me of your plan.''

''. . . less per month for the employees,'' she finished, then pushed her glasses on top of her head.

''Are there start-up costs?'' he asked as he poured them each a second glass of wine.

''Some, but nothing outrageous. The agent tried to soft-shoe me into going for something more expensive, but I refused to budge.''

''You're turning into quite a tycoon. Pretty soon you'll have the company listed on the stock exchange.''

''Hardly.'' She sipped from her glass. ''But I am enjoying my work. More than I thought I would.''

''You've done well.'' He surprised himself by meaning the compliment.

In the last few weeks, Amy had tamed the paper tiger in his office and reduced the chaos to a manageable level. The employees liked and respected her, and so did he. If only he could convince his body that he had no place in her bed.

''I'm glad you think so,'' she said. ''Because after I get my new assistant trained, I'm going to computerize the scheduling.''

He groaned. ''I don't want to hear about it. If I'm not careful, you'll have me carrying around a date book.''

''Oh, what a great idea. Then you'd never have an excuse to forget dinner with the family.''

''That remark does not deserve a response.'' He stood up. ''Under our agreement, I believe it is your turn to clean up. So, if you'll excuse me, I have to take a shower.''

"Another one?"

"Yes. I'm going out."

"Oh." The laughter in her eyes faded. "H–have a good time."

He wanted to tell her he was just meeting a few of his friends on a boat, but held back. Better for her to think he was seeing another woman. Better for both of them.

"A–my. What's happenin', boss lady?" Bob leaned over the side of the powerboat and grinned. "Any bonuses for hard-working employees?"

"Nothing this week," she said as she crossed the dock. "Are you varnishing again?"

He nodded. "Yeah, every quarter. It's the only crummy side of the job, ya know."

"And you scrub down every boat, every week?"

"Sure. Salt water's real corrosive. It eats away at the finish if we don't."

She tapped her foot a couple of times. "How long will it take you to finish this boat?"

"Four days."

"You're kidding?"

"Nope. But I'm a fast worker." He puffed out his chest like a proud peacock. The action looked peculiar on a man wearing a T-shirt with a logo that stated, *I'm a champion beer drinker*. "Joe would take at least a week."

"Thanks for the information. Do you know when Mac's due back?"

"About four."

"Great. Thanks." She started up the ramp toward the office.

Once inside, she made a beeline for her desk and began searching for the pamphlets. In the last month, three companies had approached Spirno Marine about taking over the washing and varnishing of the boats. Using their figures, she quickly worked up a cost analysis.

When Julie, her new assistant, returned from lunch, the two women completed the task. By three-thirty, the printer had produced the final report.

"What do you think?" Amy asked.

"It's wonderful," Julie answered. The petite redhead was in her early twenties. She'd taken the job after a divorce had left her solely responsible for two small children. She and Amy had worked out a flex-time schedule that left the office covered more than eight hours a day and Julie's child care bills at a minimum. "I think Mac'll be really impressed."

"I'm not so sure." Amy folded the sheets together. "I hope he doesn't think I'm butting in where I don't belong." She smiled quickly. "Wish me luck."

"You'll be fine."

Julie's words of encouragement kept her spirits high all the way to the end of the dock. But as she paced back and forth, waiting for the red and white powerboat to come into view, she began to have second thoughts.

A speedboat raced back to the dock. As the wake hit, she automatically bent her knees and compensated for the shifting in the planks. Kids, she thought with a grin, then laughed out loud. She'd sure come a long way from that scared woman of two months before.

The sound of a powerful diesel engine caught her attention. Up ahead, the forty-five-foot cabin cruiser slowed, then drifted gently into the slip. Sunburned fishermen assisted with the docking, then proudly carried off the ice chests containing their catch.

"How did it go, gentlemen?" she asked as they walked past.

The leader of the group, a short man with a beer belly, grinned. "Caught a twenty pounder, ma'am. Don't see 'em like that everyday."

His buddies jabbed him in the ribs. "Twenty pounds, Ron? More like two."

"I'm telling you, that fish is twenty pounds. Maybe twenty-five . . ."

She watched to make sure they made their way safely to the parking lot, then turned back to Mac. "Hi."

He pulled off his baseball cap and ran his hand through his hair. "Hi, yourself. I don't usually get a welcome. What's the occasion?"

"Just something I want to talk to you about. But I can wait until you get everything put away."

"Did you eat lunch? There's still sandwiches."

"Okay."

She moved to the side of the boat, then stepped on board. The large craft bobbed slightly.

"Let's go below. I've had enough sun for today." He led the way.

She followed, allowing her gaze to linger on his broad shoulders. The T-shirt, bleached by a combination of elements and time, had faded to a pale blue. The cloth clung tightly, defining the hard muscles that rippled as he moved. Farther down, tanned, firm legs bulged and released as he walked.

A drop of perspiration trickled between her breasts. She suspected it had nothing to do with the weather.

"Have a seat."

She slid onto the bench and took the soda he offered. The powerboats were wider than the sailboats. Their interiors were more open and luxurious, with sofas and wine racks and expensive carpeting. Wide windows looked out onto the dock and ocean. From the corner of her eye, she could see the queen-sized bed that filled the master suite. Did he ever . . .

She pushed the thought away.

"What do you want to talk about?" he asked as he unwrapped a sandwich and passed her half.

"The boats. I've been thinking a lot about the cleaning and varnishing we do. It's time consuming. Do you know it takes Bob four days to do one? That's four days that Bob and the boat aren't out with clients."

Mac took a bite and shrugged. "Can't be helped," he said when he'd finished chewing. "Varnishing's a fact of life in the marine business. Everybody has the same problem."

"Not exactly." She opened the spreadsheet. "I've worked out the costs for us to do the work ourselves. It would be cheaper to hire it out."

Placing the half-eaten sandwich on the table, he glanced outside. "You don't know what you're talking about, princess. It's not that simple. There's more to the job than saving money. You have to worry about the quality of varnish and how the job's done. Stick to reorganizing the office and leave the boats to me."

"But Mac, if you'd just take a look at what I've done . . ."

"No." His voice was flat.

"But . . ."

"I mean it, Amy. Stay out."

"Why are you being so pigheaded?"

"Why are you working on things that don't concern you?"

She slid off the bench and stood up. "I'm your partner, Mac. Stop treating me like some bimbo."

He glared at her. "Look, Amy—"

The rage in his eyes made her want to run for cover, but she stood her ground. This crisis had been coming for a long time, she thought.

Ever since Mac had told her he believed women took whatever they wanted, she'd half-suspected he thought that of her. It hurt to know he didn't trust her, but this was as good a time as any to lay their cards on the table. "No, *you* look. I've got some important information here. I won't be put off because you want to play the omnipotent sea captain. I'm not Jenny. I'm not going to take anything away from you."

He acted as if she'd punched him in the chest. The stiff lines of his face sharpened in surprise, then froze, while he took a step back. "Why don't you say what you really mean?"

"I'm an equal partner. Therefore, half of everything is my responsibility. I think it's time I learned about the boats and chartering. I'm not interested in being the leader or any of that nonsense, but I'm tired of you keeping me locked up in that office. I'm not stupid. I'm capable of contributing, yet if you restrict me to filing memos, you're doing both me and the business a disservice."

She held her breath and waited for the explosion. There was only silence.

He walked to the window and stared out at the sea. Would he throw her out? Would she have to find another job? Twisting her hands together, she studied the unyielding line of his back. Come on, Mac, she pleaded silently. Give us both a chance.

"When did you grow up?" he asked quietly.

She exhaled with relief. "Sometime in the last two months."

"I guess I wasn't paying attention." Mac turned back to face her. His dark eyes were filled with concern, apprehension, and a grudging respect. "You sure you want to be a full partner?"

She nodded.

"That means going out on the ocean. You ready to test your sea legs again?"

"I've been reading up on sea sickness. Some of it is caused by an imbalance in the inner ear. The rest is a result of nerves. I think I had a combination of the two. If I can learn to relax, sea sickness medication would probably take care of the rest."

He strolled back to the bench and sat down. "There are day rentals and fishing charters. You'll need to learn about equipment, bait, and locations. Then, there's cleaning the fish for the clients."

She tasted bile in her throat and grimaced. "Go on."

"Overnight and several-day charters. You'll need a sea captain's license. We can start with the six-pack license and work up. There's navigation, charts, equipment, rules of the road. You up to this, princess?"

He exuded power and confidence. It filled the cabin and made her restless. The sculpted lines of his face highlighted his strength. She wanted him . . . but not just for tonight . . . she wanted him for always. But before she could begin to think about taming a man like Mac, she had to conquer her own demons.

"Yes," she said clearly. "I'm ready."

He took a long drink of soda, then set the can on the table. "A four-hour fishing trip leaves tomorrow at one. Be on the dock at noon and you can help me set up." He glanced at her skirt and blouse. "Wear deck shoes, shorts, and a T-shirt. You'll need a hat and plenty of sunscreen. Eat a light lunch."

Relief was the first reaction. The second was a voice asking if she was crazy. She'd received everything she'd asked for. Now, it was up to her to make it work.

She saluted. "Aye, aye, captain."

His grin filled her like a hot coal dropped inside her heart. The heat built, then exploded into a flash fire of sensation.

"I'll go over your report and we'll discuss it in a couple of days. I sure hope you know what you're doing, Amy."

She backed from the salon and moved toward the relative safety of the dock. "Me, too."

"Ready to go?" Mac asked as he lowered an ice chest over the side of the cabin cruiser.

"You bet." Amy took the fishing poles Bob offered and stepped on board. "Did I dress appropriately?"

Mac's eyes followed the length of her. From the top of her baseball cap to the tip of her new white deck shoes, she was as alluring as a sea nymph and twice as dangerous.

The hat was the exact blue of her eyes. Wisps of her bangs pressed flat against her forehead, while tufts of blonde hair stuck out by her ears and over her neck. A single white stripe of zinc oxide protected her nose from the sun. Her cheeks flushed with what seemed to be equal parts of excitement and apprehension. Shiny lips turned up in an irresistible smile. Part beautiful woman, part successful businesswoman, she was the best of both worlds.

His gaze dropped. The pink tank top left honey-colored arms bare. The knit fabric clung to and emphasized every luscious curve. Light shorts ended a scant inch below her crotch, exposing more tanned skin. He felt a rumbling inside. It had nothing to do with missing lunch.

"Well, captain?" she asked, shifting her weight from one foot to the other. "Do I pass inspection?"

The only thing the fishermen would be interested in catching was her, he thought. "You're perfect," he said, trying to ignore the husky quality of his voice.

Extending his right index finger, he traced a line from her shoulder to her wrist. She was warm and soft. Some part of him, apart from the detached demeanor he wore like armor plating, noted the slight tremor rippling across her skin. It would be so easy to take her here . . . on the boat. Just a few feet away was a wide bed with crisp cotton sheets. The refrigerator contained enough food to get them through an entire weekend of loving. He could cast off and take them far out to sea. With only the ocean and the wind and the stars, they could find their way to a place that had no reality, save that of mouths and tongues and bodies connected and consumed in an ever-raging fire. He moved closer.

"Where do you want the bait, boss?" Bob asked as he stepped on board.

"Is it live?"

"Of course."

"Fill up the bait well." Mac stepped back and pointed to the built-in containers by the stern, then smiled at Amy. "Why don't I show you the charts and you can see where we're going. There are various reports that tell us where the fish are. Depending on the type of client and how long they've chartered the boat for, we determine the best place to go."

He opened the wide drawer and pulled out the appropriate sheets. Amy glanced up at him, her big eyes dark with unasked questions.

I don't know either, he thought to himself. This wanting between them wasn't going away. But he hadn't forgotten his promise and he was still doing his damnedest to keep his distance. The world was filled with men who wanted a sweet, beautiful loving woman at their side. God knows, he was one of them. But unlike the unnamed masses, he knew his limitations. As he'd been told a hundred times, he was simply a rebel and incapable of being the man Amy needed, no, deserved.

He spread the chart flat and tried to ignore the subtle scent of her perfume. "Here's the marina," he said, indicating the appropriate place on the chart. "We're going out to about here. It's going to take an hour to get there and . . ."

When the last fisherman had boarded, Mac smiled at Amy. "This is your last chance to back out, princess."

She shook her head. "No way. I'm ready." She patted her shorts' pocket. "Extra-strength motion sickness medicine. I'll be fine."

"Then cast off."

She walked to the bow of the boat and untied the line. After tossing it to Bob on the dock, she turned and gave Mac a thumb's up. "All clear, captain."

The powerful twin diesel engines accelerated. The vibration under Mac's feet was steady and normal. In the back, four men chatted among themselves, arguing about lures and bait, line weight, and who would catch the most fish.

Amy slipped below and began loading up a tray with sandwiches. They provided food and drink for the fishermen, although alcohol was limited to beer. Mac'd had his fill of drunks at sea and he didn't allow them on his boats.

"Bar's open, gentlemen," he called above the sound of the engine and the waves. "Help yourself." Hitting a button on the side of the console, he started a tape. Upbeat rock music added to the general cacophony.

When Amy had passed out the food, she joined him at the helm. The boat was designed with a large rear deck that made it perfect for fishing. A high fighting chair could be bolted down to assist with the catch. Benches lined the square area. The overhead canvas, currently rolled up, could be pulled out for shade or protection from the elements.

The flying bridge was slightly above the rear deck. As Amy climbed the steps, she balanced two sodas in one hand and a sandwich in the other.

"You're not eating?" he asked as he patted the bench next to his chair.

"I thought I'd have a bite of yours, but that's all. I don't want to risk anything." She took a seat and handed him the food.

"How are you doing?"

"So far, so good."

The boat cleared the last buoy of the marina and he headed southeast. After popping open his drink and hanging it in the holder, he pushed both throttles open. "Hang on. This is where we separate the men from the boys."

The powerful craft leapt forward, skimming over the crests of the waves. The up and down motion decreased considerably. Salty spray splashed over the bow and deposited droplets on his arms and face.

Amy grinned. "This isn't so bad," she shouted over the noise. "Can I steer?"

"Sure. Keep to this heading. I'll eat. Watch out for smaller boats."

They changed places. Mac glanced behind them to check on the passengers; the men were lost in their own conversation. He unwrapped the sandwich.

"Tear me off a corner, please," Amy called. "I want to take another pill."

"I thought you took one already."

"I did. I want to make sure."

"Don't tell your mother I've turned you into a motion sickness medicine junkie."

She turned to him and laughed. The affectionate sound threatened to drown him in a pool of loving concern. He'd never wanted a woman as much as he wanted her; the need was slowly killing him.

The food turned to sawdust in his mouth, but he forced himself to keep eating. Not by a whisper would he let Amy know how he felt. She was still off-limits to the likes of him.

He'd always known she'd had a crush on him. When she was sixteen, it had been easy to read the adoration in her eyes. But he refused to capitalize on whatever emotions might linger. Amy was here to make a fresh start; she didn't need a guy like him hanging around and messing up her plans. Whatever decision she made about the partnership, he was willing to accept. Even though it meant never claiming her as his own.

"Are you done eating?" she asked, interrupting his reverie.

He nodded.

"I'm going below to get another drink. Do you want anything?"

"No."

She gave him a quick hug and a kiss on the cheek. "I'm having a great time, Mac. Thanks for letting me be a part of all this."

"Save your gratitude until after you've gutted the fish."

"You wouldn't."

"I would . . . and I will."

She swatted his arm. "Beast!"

"That's what all the ladies tell me, although they usually say it with a smile."

After she disappeared below, he stared out over the ocean. He'd always thought of hell as a forbidding place of pain and destruction. Now he knew it was living in the same house with Amy, wanting and needing the one woman he could never have.

They reached the fishing area about forty minutes later. Mac slowed the boat and went down to make sure the men were getting their gear together. He hadn't seen Amy since she'd disappeared to get another soda.

Slowly, he stepped down into the cabin. Don't let her be sick, he thought. That was the last thing either of them needed. But she wasn't curled up in the head. Instead, he found her stretched out on the forward bunk. Her hat had rolled off the mattress and onto the carpet. One arm stretched out to the side, the other was tucked under her sleeping body.

He smiled. Too much medication. She was such a lightweight. After pulling a thin blanket over her back, he reached down and brushed the hair out of her eyes. "Sleep tight, princess."

Amy rolled over and stretched. Boy, she'd really been tired. Rubbing her eyes, she pushed up to a sitting position. Why was her mattress rocking?

Her eyes flew open. This wasn't her bedroom. This wasn't even Mac's house. The lavish decor looked familiar, but she couldn't quite figure out . . .

" 'Bout time you decided to join the living."

"M–Mac?" She cleared her throat. "What happened?"

"You took one too many of your little pills and fell asleep."

There was a vague recollection of being overwhelmed by the need to stretch out for just a second. She'd climbed onto the bunk and . . .

"Oh! I only took the recommended dosage." Heat climbed up her cheeks. "You must think I'm a real pain."

"Something like that."

"Are we still at sea?"

"Nope. Back in the marina. The men left about a half hour ago."

Her eyes flew to her watch. "How long have I been asleep?"

"About five hours."

She hung her head. "Do you hate me?"

"No."

The mattress dipped as he sat next to her. His dark

eyes were filled with amusement and affection. These were the times, she thought. Moments stolen between the realities of their lives, when she let herself believe it could all be real. That the demons had been put to rest and they were simply a man and a woman who cared for and respected one another. Emotion filled her until she felt compelled to identify the feeling. But before she could, she became aware of him so close by.

In the small confines of the cabin, she could smell the salt air lingering on his skin. His bare legs were inches from her hand and it took every bit of willpower to keep from caressing the powerful limbs.

It had to be the lingering effects of sleep, she told herself firmly. There was no other explanation for her sudden urge to pull him down next to her and discover all that she'd simply dreamed about.

"I've been thinking about our arrangement."

She looked at him. "Oh, Mac, don't lock me back in the office. I'll do better next time."

One long finger touched her chin. It was like standing too close to a flame. "No one's going to lock you up anywhere. I've decided that we're going about this the wrong way. I tend to go full speed ahead without thinking of the consequences. If you want to learn about this side of the business, we should start with the basics."

"What does that mean."

He stood up. "Meet me at seven o'clock tonight, by the pool. Dress for swimming."

"But I don't know how to swim."

"Exactly." He walked toward the galley, then turned back. "And, Amy?"

"Yes?"

"For my sake . . . Don't wear a bikini."

SEVEN

Amy clutched her short terrycloth robe more firmly around her body. This is silly, she told herself as she tiptoed toward the backyard. She was just going swimming. There was no reason to feel as if she were about to be publicly exposed. Ted had seen her in a lot less and she'd never felt this nervous. Calm down.

But the upbeat pep talk didn't even begin to still the thundering of her heart. Her palms were sweaty and her mouth was dry. She was afraid of the water and knew, without a doubt, she was about to make an incredible fool of herself in front of the one person she would most like to impress.

Pulling open the sliding glass door, she paused, then stepped onto the patio. Soft lamps chased away the evening's shadows and created pockets of light. Mac was already in the pool, swimming the length with slow, lazy strokes. The blue water illuminated him from below, making the up and down motion of his legs clearly visible. Part of her admired the corded strength, part of her wanted to run for Kansas.

He stood up in the shallow end and saw her. "Right on time. Ready for your first lesson?"

"I—I guess."

"Don't be nervous. I'm not going to make you do anything you don't want to do. We'll take it as slow as you need to." He smiled, his white teeth flashing brilliantly in the evening. "My supply of patience is endless."

Unbidden, a delicious thought wove its way into her brain. Was he so very accommodating in bed? When the sheets were tangled and the wanting overwhelming, did he still draw upon that endless well of patience?

He held out his hand. "Come on, Amy. I won't let anything happen to you."

Taking a breath for courage, she dropped her robe on the ground and stepped into the pool. The water was pleasantly warm, lapping first at her ankles, then knees, then thighs. When she touched the bottom of the shallow end, she ducked under, then stood up.

No bikini, he'd said. Not a problem. She hadn't owned one in years. The blue scrap of lycra she was wearing had seemed conservative enough in the department store dressing room, but now, with Mac moving closer and closer, she resisted the urge to tug up at the bodice or down at the bottom.

He loomed large in the darkness. Individual features were caught, then escaped the dim light. He was tall and broad and male . . . and virtually naked. Drops of water clung to the hair on his chest; they reflected the lamps like individual prisms. Below, his long legs were highlighted in the clear liquid. She felt small and insignificant next to him.

The hunger began. She recognized the symptoms; God knows they'd kept her awake enough times in the past two months. An achy feeling started low in her belly, then radiated out. Skin, suddenly sensitized by need, prickled with anticipation. Her breathing quickened. Let him think it was fear.

"Have you ever tried to swim?" Mac asked.

"A couple of times. I can float on my back."

"Good." He grinned and moved to the left. "Show me."

The lesson progressed slowly. After she proved her proficiency at floating, he taught her the correct kicking motion. Then came the arms. His hands demonstrated, but never touched. Frustration grew until it threatened to suffocate her with its heavy presence.

She glanced up at the sky. Clouds chased across the vast darkness, hiding the moon and covering the stars. A slight breeze picked up and the air seemed damp.

"Now, let's put the two motions together," Mac said.

Amy let go of the edge of the pool and stood up. "You mean, swim?"

"That *is* why we're here. Come on." He took her hand and pulled her to the wall. "Try it across the shallow end. I'll hold on to you. If you get scared, just stand up. You'll be fine."

She pushed her wet hair out of her eyes and drew a deep breath. One of Mac's arms wrapped around her middle, just above her waist, the other pushed against her back. Gritting her teeth against the fear, she struck out, gamely kicking with her legs and paddling with her hands. Before she could think about standing up, they'd reached the opposite side.

"I did it." She looked back over the distance she'd traveled. "That wasn't so bad. Let's try it again."

"That's my girl." His eyes sent her a message of pride at her accomplishment.

She savored the encouragement, all the while trying to ignore the warm arm inches from her throbbing breasts. Maybe if she took off her bathing suit he'd get the message. Before she could consider her plan, he was urging her to swim again.

On the fourth crossing, he took his arm away. She felt it the instant the support was removed. For a second, she floundered, then Mac's voice steadied her and she continued to the side.

He pulled her into a quick, wet hug, then set her on her feet. "I knew you could do it."

"Thanks." She drew in a breath, her panting brought on as much by the close contact with his near-naked body as by the swimming itself. "I can't believe I did it by myself."

"Ready for the next test?" he asked.

"Why don't I like that question?"

He pulled her toward the steps and urged her out of the pool. "We'll try swimming the length now. We start at the deep end. By the time you think about getting scared, you'll be able to stand up."

They walked around, then she sat on the edge of the deep end and dangled her feet in the water. "Maybe I'm already scared."

"I know you can do this."

"Yeah, right."

He dove into the pool and came up by her feet.

"Lower yourself down. I'll hold on to you. When you're ready, let go of the side and start swimming. I'll be right in front of you the whole way."

When he looked at her with that expression that said he believed in her, she couldn't bear to let him down. "Whose idea was this anyway?" she grumbled as she slipped into the liquid depths.

Panic threatened when her feet encountered nothing, but she stared at Mac. "Help!"

"It's okay, princess." He brushed her cheek, then swam back two strokes and treaded water. "You can do it. Come to me."

He watched her swallow, then strike out. Her blue eyes never left his. Stroke by stroke, she moved forward. Gradually, determination replaced the fear. She was a hell of a woman, he thought as his feet touched the bottom and he continued to lead her to the end of the pool.

Teaching her to swim had been a great idea in theory. If he'd given a moment's thought to the unique torture of being so close, but unable to touch her—really touch her—he would have sent her to Hawaii for lessons. Even now, he could still feel the rapid beating of her heart when he had held her level as she learned the strokes. The brush of their bare legs as she had kicked, the memory of repositioning her hands—all wore him down like water carving granite.

His back bumped into the cement lip of the decking. She swam until she was inches from him, then stood up. "I did it!"

Without warning, she flung her arms around his neck. He could feel her breasts flatten against his chest, the beaded nubs of her nipples grinding deliciously on his skin. Pulling her closer, he lifted her off the bottom and spun with her in his arms. Her legs wrapped around his hips as she clung tightly. Her face nestled in the curve between his neck and shoulder. Warm puffs of air danced across his flesh.

The water lapped sensuously against his thighs. One hand slipped lower and squeezed the tender roundness of her buttock. The heat of her center radiated out through the layers of their swimsuits and surrounded the hardness pressing against her.

It would be so easy, he thought grimly. So very easy to slip down her straps and feast like a man long denied. His mouth watered at the thought of her sweetness, of each inch he would taste and savor and arouse. He longed to hear her breathing change from calm to frenzied and back again, to feel her hands grasping and loving, giving to him all that she received, to know the exact dimensions of her tight, wet core.

Cooling drops of rain fell on his head and shoulders. "The storm," he murmured, more to himself than her.

There was a slight pressure on his neck, as if a feather danced across his skin. It occurred again and again as she trailed kisses from his jaw to his collarbone.

Stop, his conscience screamed, but his engorged body answered differently. Two fingers sought the tender flesh of her thigh, tracing patterns ever closer to the elastic of her suit.

"Mac." Amy's voice was quiet and husky, as though the act of speaking was almost more than she could endure.

He released her and she slipped down until her feet were touching the bottom of the pool. One of his hands continued to rub up and down her back, the other rested on her ribs, a scant inch below her breasts. Her eyes, nearly black in the darkness of the coming storm, searched for an answer he could not allow himself to give.

He felt her fingers kneading his shoulders, then slipping lower to his chest. Electricity shot through him, echoing the bolt of lightning that cut across the sky.

"I don't object to dying in your arms," he said, turning toward the stairs. "But I'd rather not be electrocuted."

She followed him without speaking. Her desire was as plain as his—the physical proof more subtle, but no less discernible. He slipped her robe over her shoulders, then led her to the sliding glass door.

"Mac," she repeated, touching her fingers to his lips. "I want . . ."

"Shh." He bit the pads, then soothed the injury with his tongue. "Amy, I can't."

"Why?"

Because he was the biggest fool this side of the moon. Only a complete moron would turn down her passionate invitation. But he knew he didn't deserve her. The morning could only bring recriminations. He'd rather burn than see regret in her eyes for what had occurred. "I gave you my word."

She moved closer and rubbed against him. His low moan mingled with the thunder. "I never asked for your word."

"Believe me, I'm not happy either, but it's best for both of us." After opening the door, he pushed her inside and followed.

"Who died and made you king?" she asked, slipping

her arms into the sleeves of her cover-up. "You have no right to make that kind of decision for me. It's my life, Mac. You're not my mother."

"I'm also not the right man for you, princess."

"Don't call me that!" She tied the belt with a jerk. Anger had replaced the passion, but the energy burned just as bright. "I'm not a princess. I'm a plain, ordinary woman."

He touched her arm. "Never ordinary."

"Save the compliments for one of your other women." She turned away. "And I suppose this is another of those events we pretend never happened?"

"Yes."

"Fine." Stomping toward the hall, she shook her head. "I'm still weak enough to eventually forgive you, but don't expect me to cook you breakfast in the morning."

Five seconds later the slamming of her bedroom door reverberated through the house.

The storm grew louder as rain raged upon them. It stopped at three-seventeen in the morning. Mac knew the exact time. He was still awake, fighting the fantasies of what might have been.

It was three days before Amy was able to look at Mac without being torn between running for cover and cutting his heart out. It was another two weeks before they returned to their comfortable, humorous relationship. The business thrived and the swimming instructions continued, although Mac never again joined her in the pool. The first Saturday of May, he decided to move on to the next set of lessons.

"I don't want to," Amy said as he opened the car door.

"This entire project is your idea. It's a little late to get cold feet."

She tucked her purse under the front seat of the car and crossed her arms over her chest. "It's not my feet I'm worried about."

"Amy!" he growled.

"Ma–ac," she mocked back.

"Get over here."

He grabbed her arm and pulled until she was forced to go with him or be dragged across the parking lot. When they reached the top of the polished ramp, she stopped.

"I can't."

"You have to. It's required as part of your captain's license."

"Couldn't I wait for another class?"

"It doesn't start for weeks. What's the problem?"

She shrugged, not wanting to admit she was scared . . . and embarrassed. Mac tugged on her arm. Her shoes slipped a little down the ramp. He tugged again. She slid further.

"You're acting like a child," he said.

"Thank you. Then I should fit right in."

Bending slightly at the waist, she allowed him to pull her the rest of the way. When they finally reached the dock, she stared at a semicircle of half a dozen faces staring back. Let 'em look, she thought. They'd never see fear in *her* eyes.

"Hey, Mac. Good to see you, buddy." A tall blond man broke through the line and held out his hand. "This your new partner?"

While the men shook hands, the twenty-something instructor gave Amy the once-over. She bristled at the action, then smiled sweetly when she saw anger flare in Mac's eyes. Served him right, making her do this.

The young man turned to Amy. "I'm John. Welcome to the beginning sailing class."

"Thank you."

John grinned. He was as tall as Mac, but not as well built. Whereas her partner's clothes clung like barnacles to a hull, John's regulation shorts and T-shirt hung loosely.

"You're the last to arrive, so let's get started." He glanced at the group of students. "All right, boys and girls . . . and Amy, of course. Today we're going to learn about sailing. The first hour will be spent studying the various parts of a boat and then we'll all get into our crafts and sail around the harbor."

The ten-year-olds gathered around eagerly. Amy tossed Mac one more scowl and moved closer to John. She'd make Napoleon Christopher Spirno regret forcing her to take this class, if it was the last thing she ever did.

"Remember to yell 'Coming about' before tacking," John called out through the megaphone. "I know it's just you out there now, but it's a good habit to start. That way, you'll be sure to say it when you're sailing with someone else. Most people don't like being knocked overboard."

The ten-year-olds laughed uproariously, Amy noted as she struggled with her sail. But then they seemed to find everything funny. Especially her! While she foundered in the center of the harbor, they flitted about like winged, amphibious creatures. Their sails puffed out regally while she was stuck in the windless vacuum of Calcutta.

She swung the boom of her twelve-foot boat to the opposite side, praying for a whisper of a breeze. The sail hung as limply as her spirits. She blew a couple of times, but that didn't help either. The sun was warm on her back, the water sparkling, the air clear. So, why did she feel like throwing a temper tantrum?

"How's it going, Amy?" John's voice drifted across the water.

She waved. "Just peachy."

Paul, a boy with red hair and freckles, swooped past. "Move your sail to the other side, Amy. Wind's picking up."

Mutant, she thought as she followed the instructions. Instantly, a gust rippled the triangle of white cloth. "I'm moving."

"Good. Now, stay on course and when you reach the red buoy, tack to port."

"Thank you." She smiled and ignored the guilt welling up for mentally calling him names. When she reached the marker, she surreptitiously glanced at the bottom of her shoes to find the "P" for port, then swung the boom. The craft slowed for a second, then moved swiftly across the water.

The breeze seemed to shift slightly. Her sail flickered and started to sag. "No, you don't." Acting out of instinct rather than training or good sense, she pushed hard on the rudder with her right hand and pulled the line tight with her left.

Instantly, the sail filled with wind and snapped to life. She was sailing!

By the end of the third hour, Amy felt ready to take on the seven seas. She'd dodged other boats, lowered and raised her sails, even raced Paul to the far buoy and back. So what if she hadn't won, she'd still come in a close second.

A tall figure joined John at the railing. Despite the distance, she recognized Mac. Her hand slipped on the rudder and she narrowly avoided plowing into another craft.

Trying to ignore him, she circled the boat and headed toward the far end of the sailing area. He was stubborn, she thought, and a giant pain in the butt. He never let her get away with anything, he fought her on every new plan she had for the business and absolutely refused to discuss where he'd been spending his evenings. On the other hand, he was loyal to a fault, unfailingly support-ive, and a man of his word. The problems the last quality had caused brought a grim smile to her lips.

Damn him for his idealism, she thought. Women were always complaining about the number of men who were selfish jerks. Just her luck, she had to stumble upon the world's last knight in shining armor. Long live the king and hip-hip hooray for chivalry.

Loosening the sail, she held the rudder to starboard and began the wide turn back. She wanted him, there was no doubt about that. Despite his resistance to inti-macy, she burned. Knowing why he resisted didn't make the situation any easier to bear. She knew he had lofty ideals about her needs. He thought she deserved a man with qualities he didn't possess.

If only the truth were that easy. In her mind, the issue of what she should look for remained unresolved. Could she trust her judgment?

When she'd met Ted, she'd been sure they were in love. There hadn't been any of the passion she felt for Mac, but there had been a steady affection. Yet, when he had started running around with other women, she'd been more angry than hurt. The regrets she had about her marriage were the loss of the baby and that she'd married Ted at all, not that they'd broken up.

What did that mean? Was she incapable of loving? Or had she simply connected with the wrong person? Did she love Mac or was she still caught up in a school-girl crush? Had enough passed between them for her to have let go of the idol and discover the man?

The redheaded boy swooped next to her. "Don't forget, you lost the race."

She grinned. "I won't, Paul."

They docked and lowered the sails. Before Amy could step out of her craft, Mac was there, holding out his hand.

"How did it go, prin . . . pretty fine day." She glanced at him, but he just shrugged. "What can you expect? It's a hard habit to break."

"I had a wonderful time. I hope you weren't planning to go right back to the office."

"No. I thought we'd have lunch."

"Oh, boy." Paul joined them. "How about the pizza place at the end of the marina?"

Mac looked down at the kid. "Do I know you?"

"Naw. Amy and me raced, and she lost."

"Oh? And what did you race for?"

Amy grinned. "Lunch."

"For your little friend here?" Mac asked.

"Not exactly." The other kids gathered around.

"For who then, as if I didn't know."

His tone was fierce, but she saw the laughter lurking in his dark eyes. "What can I say? I'm spineless."

"Does that mean . . ."

"Yup. The entire class. And John. Hope you brought lots of cash."

"But, Amy, the Robinsons are coming and they're bringing Alfred."

"I'm sorry, Mom, but I'll be out on the boat. We have a four-day charter and, I'm part of the crew." Amy didn't know who Alfred was, but she had a real good idea she didn't want to eat dinner with him.

"But . . ."

Amy held the phone away from her ear and listened to the familiar list of complaints. Just once she'd like her mother to say she approved, or was unconditional love too much to ask from the woman who had brought her into the world?

". . . and I don't think it's a good idea for you to be captaining this vessel," the older woman continued. "You haven't had a chance to learn anything. You always were a slow learner, Amy."

She raised her eyes toward the heavens and prayed for patience. "I'm not going to be the captain, Mom. I don't have my license yet. I'm going on the trip as the cook." She heard Lynn's gasp. "And the maid."

"I . . . I . . ."

"Gotta go. Mac and I will be over for dinner next week. 'Bye."

After hanging up the phone, she sighed. Nothing was easy. Still, she'd done her best. The relationship wasn't all her responsibility. Until her mother agreed to meet her halfway, they'd never be more than superficial acquaintances. It was a regret, but one she had learned to live with.

"Ready to go?" Mac asked as he walked into the kitchen.

Amy pointed toward her packed bag. "Just waiting for you, captain."

He moved next to her and cupped her face in his hands. Warm brown eyes stared down, saying with a look what he would never allow himself to speak aloud. *I care about you, too*, she whispered in her mind. *Help me understand what it means.*

His fingers caressed her cheeks, then dropped back to his sides. "Four days, four nights, no land. Final chance for the chickens to stay on shore."

She picked up her duffel bag. "I intend to fry the chickens, not join their ranks. Last one in the car has to make the beds."

Amy walked to the end of the ramp and came to a stop. "Wow! Where did she come from?"

Mac nudged her from behind, to keep her moving. "The *Christina*'s been rented out since you got here. Isn't she a beauty?"

The sixty-five-foot motor yacht nestled against the slip, like a swan resting near shore. She was all white, with wide dark windows and a tall flying bridge. Long antennas reached for the sky.

"She's fully equipped," Mac said, hearing the pride in his own voice. "Nappy had her refurbished right before he died." He stepped on board and unlocked the rear door. "We don't usually get a lot of charters for her, so we list her with a couple of other companies. If they find the client, they get a percentage of the rental fee. Several corporations have used her for executive outings.''

"Christina?" She frowned. "Why is that name familiar?''

He looked beyond Amy to a past that was gone, but not forgotten. The memories tumbled over one another. Delicious smells drifting from an ever-open kitchen, plump arms holding him tight in a world gone mad, a soft voice mingling Greek with broken English, forming a musical speech. "She was Nappy's wife and my grandmother. She died when I was about fifteen.''

"Of course. I remember him talking about their life together." She smiled sadly. "I wish I'd known her.''

"She would have liked you. The two of you would have gotten along great." He stepped back and held open the door. "Have a look.''

While she explored the boat, he began unloading their supplies. By ten-thirty, Bob had arrived with the food and the work began in earnest.

Two couples had chartered the *Christina* for a fishing trip. The boat was fully self-contained with three levels. Up top was the bridge. The middle level contained the day quarters, with the main salon, galley, and eating areas. To the stern was the wide deck for sunning and fishing. Below were the cabins. With almost fifteen hundred gallons of fuel, they'd easily cruise through the Keys and out in the Gulf. Once they'd left port, they wouldn't dock again for ninety-six hours.

Amy appeared beside him, her face flushed with excitement. "She's wonderful. Have you seen the master suite? It's huge." She laughed. "For a boat, anyway. Where do we sleep?''

"There's guest quarters below, but you might be more comfortable up top."

She climbed the ladder to the bridge deck and leaned over the rail. "On the floor?"

He nodded. "Bob and I will take turns on watch. There's usually a nice breeze. The fresh air will keep your tummy from acting up. I brought an extra sleeping bag. It's up to you."

He wasn't sure why, but he seemed to be waiting on pins and needles for her answer. Maybe it was because the boat was a different dimension, separated in space and time from the real world. Here he could allow himself to imagine all that would never be . . . a future with Amy. For these few nights, they could sleep side by side, enjoying a closeness that, on land, propriety and his good sense denied them. With Bob standing by on watch, there was no risk of anything getting out of hand. It was simply a new way to torture himself.

"Okay," she said, ducking under the canvas cover and backing down the ladder. When she reached his side, she smiled. "I'd better get to work. I understand the captain on this trip is a real bear to work with."

"I hear that, man." Bob set a case of sodas on the floor and wiped his face. "No time for fun on this cruise." He leaned toward Amy and grinned. "The crew meets to talk about mutiny at five."

Mac turned away. "Any disobedience will be severely punished. Don't make me lock you two in the brig."

Amy laughed. "Oh, I just love it when he talks tough."

Amy stopped by briefly to bring him dinner, but was

kept busy until almost nine. When the stars were beginning their nightly journey across the sky, she appeared silently at his side.

After checking the autopilot, he stood up and moved to the lounge bench against the bulkhead and pulled her down next to him.

"Tired?" he asked.

"Mmm, you bet." She collapsed bonelessly. "Who would have thought this little cruise would be so much work? By the time I got the cabins ready, I had to start cooking." She smiled, her teeth flashing white in the darkness. "As you know, I don't usually prepare a four-course meal."

"It was great."

"Yeah, I saw you sneaking in the galley for leftovers."

"I am the captain. Rank has its privileges."

She yawned, then leaned against him. Of its own accord, his arm shifted to hold her tight and she snuggled closer.

The motor rumbled as the boat moved through the sea. The sound of the stereo below drifted up around them. But the loudest noise was the pounding of his heart. Tension stretched the lines of his self-control to the breaking point, but he hung on to sanity. There were too many people around; he couldn't take Amy here. Besides, he'd given his word.

"Did you really like dinner?" she asked, her voice muffled against his T-shirt.

"It was delicious. I'm impressed. I didn't know you cooked French food."

"A legacy from my mother. She insisted." Amy yawned. "I'm so tired."

He pushed her upright. "I'll put out your sleeping bag. You should get some rest. Dawn comes early at sea. And it'll be your turn to be in charge."

Amy would spend much of the trip learning about Mac's duties. She would be responsible for the course, finding the fish, and assisting with the catch. He and Bob would provide the midday meals. Hot dogs and burgers, Amy had scoffed. Mac recalled the contents of the refrigerator. She was right.

"I think I will turn in, but I'll grab a snack first. Do you want something?"

Just you, he thought as the need heated the blood bubbling through his body. "Bring me whatever you're having. Oh, how's the seasickness?"

She paused in the act of stepping down the ladder and grinned. "I haven't had a moment to think about it. I even forgot to take my medication." She laughed. "It's a miracle."

At two in the morning, he left Bob at the helm and crept back to the open deck. Amy was sound asleep on top of her sleeping bag. The thick material was too heavy for a warm June night. A nylon coated blanket kept off the moisture.

He crouched beside her and gently brushed the hair from her face. So beautiful . . . so innocent. She trusted him and that was enough to cause him to keep his distance. He wouldn't betray her for the world. And yet . . .

The urge was strong. Without thinking about the potential repercussions of his action, he unrolled his sleeping bag next to hers and stretched out, careful that no part of them touched.

There was a slight stirring, then she raised up on one elbow. "Mac? Is that you?"

"Hush. It's late. Go back to sleep."

She rolled to face him. "I'm glad you're here."

Her eyes, not fully open, gazed at him. Adoration, desire, and affection mingled to form an irresistible magnet. He wanted to hold her . . . just for one night.

"Turn over," he said gruffly.

When she complied, he pulled her back until they were touching. From shoulder to calf, flesh warmed flesh. Her perfume soothed him as much as it aroused. One arm looped around her ribs, his hand fitting perfectly under her breast. The curve of her buttocks pressed against the heat of his groin. Wanting grew until the throbbing need threatened to rob him of sleep, but he was still, savoring at sea what would be denied him on land. Until the dawn, she was his.

EIGHT

Amy woke slowly. From the angle of the sun shining in her face, she knew it was time to get up and start breakfast. Not just yet, she thought, as she wiggled closer to the warm man at her side.

Without even glancing at him, she knew exactly what Mac would look like. His hair would be sticking up and his arms resting loosely at his sides. He slept like he lived: with easy grace and control. She rested her head on his shoulder and sighed.

It was the last morning. In a couple of hours, they'd pull into the slip and return to their regular lives. No more nights of waiting for him to lie down next to her and hold her close. No more dawns spent studying the lashes fanning his cheeks or the first gray hair encroaching on his temple. No more listening to the steady beat of his heart or gazing longingly at the man that could never be hers.

Holding her fingertips a scant breath above his chest,

she traced the long powerful lines. "I want you," she murmured to the sleeping man. "Not as a little girl, but as a woman."

She heard footsteps and glanced over her shoulder. Bob leaned down and grinned. "Yo, it's six-thirty," he whispered.

"Thanks."

She stood up and crept to the ladder. "Breakfast at eight. I'm making crepes."

Bob winked. "All right! I'll tell the bossman when he wakes up."

Mac sat up. "The bossman is awake. You're about as quiet as a bull in a china shop."

Amy bit her lip. How long had Mac been faking sleep? Had he heard her whispered declaration? Slowly, she raised her head and met his eyes. The dark irises gave nothing away. "How about some coffee?" he asked.

"Sure." She backed down the ladder. Had he really been asleep or had he preferred to ignore an invitation which—for him—held no appeal?

"I simply can't believe you used grandmere's recipe on that boat trip." Lynn took another sip of her wine.

No doubt she wanted to frown, Amy thought with catty superiority, but she'd never risk the wrinkles. "The guests were very impressed."

"Yeah, Amy wowed them with her cooking." Mac leaned across the table and patted her hand. "I can see she's going to be after a raise soon."

"You mean, I'm supposed to be getting paid for my job?" She winked at Mac's father. "And all this time, I've been working for free."

The four of them were eating dinner in the smaller of the family home's two dining rooms. The leaves had been pulled from the walnut table, reducing it to an intimate size, but the vastness of the room itself was intimidating. Dark oil paintings stole the light from the heavy chandelier. Thick drapes covered the windows and shut out the moon.

Mac's father, the judge, took up the conversation, giving a witty account of his last case on the bench. He was barely past sixty, with the thick dark hair and slender build of a much younger man. If she looked closely, she could see hints of Nappy's strong features. It was funny how the judge looked less like his father, while Mac was practically a younger, mirror image of the old man.

The judge had always been kind to her. Whatever trouble he'd had with his own son, he'd been willing to take the time to make an awkward teen-ager feel welcome. While they'd never been as close as she and Nappy, they'd come to care about one another.

The judge had met her mother when Amy was barely fourteen. Their courtship and subsequent marriage had been a godsend. At last, the big house had become a home. Even the boarding schools had ceased to bother her, now that she knew vacations would be spent with her new stepfather, visiting Nappy, and, of course, the wishful waiting for a visit from Mac. The good humor and strength she admired in Mac was a quality evident in all three generations of Spirno men.

". . . about three more months. The business is doing very well," Mac concluded.

The judge turned to Amy. "I understand you're responsible for a good portion of that success. You see,

Lynn, I've always said Amy had a good head on her shoulders.''

"Of course, dear.'' Lynn dismissed the information. "Amy, we're having a little dinner party next week. I'd like you to attend. There will be several suitable young men for you to meet.'' She glanced at her stepson. "You, too, Mac. Although I must warn you, Jenny will be here with her husband.''

Amy looked at him from under her lashes. The stiff lines in his face and shoulders spoke of his tension, but his voice betrayed none of the emotion. "Thanks, Lynn. I'll check my calendar and get back to you.''

"Did you know Jenny had another baby? It was just three months ago and she's already back at work. I saw her when I stopped by to have lunch with your father. I don't know how she does it. Her waist is as tiny as it ever was. She was such a lovely girl. It's too bad . . .'' She sighed delicately and motioned for the judge to pour her more wine.

Amy resisted the urge to kick her mother under the table. Did she ever stop to think that Mac might not want to hear about his ex-wife?

"Lynn, there's no need to feel badly for what happened. Jenny and I couldn't work things out between us. I wish her happiness.''

The judge leaned forward. "You sound very casual, Napoleon. Don't you want a wife and a family?''

Amy felt Mac wince at the use of his real name. He picked up his glass and drained it in one gulp. "As you've reminded me countless times, I'm not good husband material.'' Tossing his napkin on the table, he rose. "If you'll excuse me, I'll go take a walk. Amy, let me know when you're ready to leave.''

The three of them were silent as Mac walked from the room.

The judge glanced at Amy. "Tell me what I do wrong. Every time that boy and I are in the same room, we butt heads."

"I think the problem is you're too much alike."

"Amy," Lynn said sternly. "How dare you imply that my husband is anything like that . . . that . . ."

"Yes? What has Mac done that is so terrible? He didn't go to law school. That's not a crime." Amy pointed to the judge. "You didn't follow in your father's footsteps, either. Nappy wanted you to come into the family business and you wouldn't."

The older Spirno looked startled. "I never thought of it in quite those terms before."

"Well, you should. I don't mean to hurt your feelings, but if anyone is at fault here, it's you. You've told Mac he's not responsible for so long, he's started to believe you. You know I care about you, but I . . ." She felt pressure flaring up behind her eyes and stood up. "Excuse me."

The judge squeezed her arm, then let her race past him.

The long hall stretched endlessly, but there was no sign of Mac. She checked the library and the game room, then tried the front porch. All were still and empty. On her return trip, she encountered her mother.

"There you are," Lynn said, motioning for her to follow her. "I want to talk to you."

Amy reluctantly stepped into her mother's office. The room was small, compared with the rest of the house. Elegant antique furniture hid the Persian rug. Paintings, one an old master, hung on the subdued walls.

Lynn perched on the edge of a delicate Queen Anne chair and pointed to the settee opposite. "Have you quite recovered from your outburst?"

"Yes."

"It is to the judge's credit that he was not angered by your display. I, myself, would be cross, but I believe I understand your unusual expression of emotion."

"Oh." Amy looked down and realized her hands were twisting together nervously. Damn. She had spent less than two hours in the house, but she could feel herself becoming a child again. No! she thought. She was strong. She'd spent the last three months proving she could do anything she set her mind to. One evening spent in the house where she'd grown up wasn't going to undermine all that hard work.

"Yes." Lynn leaned forward, her perfectly manicured hands resting on the arms of the chair. "You think you're in love with Mac. The relationship would never work."

The older woman went on with her speech about unsuitability, but Amy got stuck on the first sentence. "You're in love with Mac."

It echoed over and over in her mind. Could it be? Was it possible that she loved, truly loved him, as a woman loves a man? And if she did, was there a chance for happiness or would Mac stubbornly resist, claiming he wasn't right for her?

"Amy, have you heard a word I've said?"

"Not really."

"Then I shall repeat myself. You must get out of this situation. Mac is not the right man for you."

Amy laughed out loud. "That's exactly what he thinks, Mom. How interesting that you should at last agree on something." Unfortunately, it was the one thing that could break her heart.

"I don't understand your cavalier attitude about this, young lady. I'm trying to explain . . ."

"Mom, do you love me?"

Lynn froze in the act of speaking, her mouth hanging open slightly. After closing her lips, she cleared her throat and glanced uneasily around the room. "I love all my children."

The question had been unexpected, but now Amy had to know. "No. Do you love *me*?"

Lynn was a slight woman, with delicate features and bones. Amy had inherited her height, along with her hair color and most of her personality, from her father. Only her eyes were the same shade of blue as the other women in the family. Now, as her mother looked up at her, she watched the color darken to indigo.

"Of course, I do. Why would you even ask?"

Amy felt a tightening in her chest. "I always wondered. I never seem to do anything to please you."

"Oh, Amy." Lynn tapped her foot impatiently, then sniffed and moved to the settee. Gathering her daughter stiffly in her arms, she awkwardly patted her back. "You have pleased me. It's just that you're so different. I've never known quite what to do with you."

She leaned against her mother and inhaled the expensive scent of the older woman's perfume. The fragrance reminded her of lectures about better grades and inappropriate behavior. The past was filled with pain, but perhaps, if they both tried a little harder, there could be something better in the future.

"You don't have to *do* anything. Just let me be myself. I have to make my own choices—Mother."

"Oh, Amy." Lynn straightened and blinked several times. "It's much too late to change your form of address. Besides, I've grown rather fond of you calling me mom."

They smiled at each other, then glanced away, unsure how to deal with the change in their relationship. Amy found herself hoping she and her mother could finally be friends.

"I don't know how I feel about Mac," she said. "But I need the time to find out. Please don't pressure me to quit my job or live somewhere else."

"I'll try, but I don't make any promises. After twenty-four years of making your decisions for you, it'll be difficult to let go."

"Mom?"

"Yes, dear?"

"I'm twenty-eight."

Amy found Mac sitting alone on the beach. The wide backyard changed from grass to sand gradually, the thick blades of green becoming more and more sparse as the coarse grains drained the nutrients from the soil.

At first, she only saw a dark shadow, barely discernible in the faint moonlight. Then the shadow moved and she recognized the broad shoulders and proud set of his head.

Her mother's words returned to haunt her. "You're in love with Mac." Was it true?

She wouldn't find out the answer standing behind him like a sniveling coward. Go on and talk to him, one side of her urged. Ask him how he feels. But her feet were glued to the ground, her legs frozen with fear. She'd rather face a hurricane at sea than risk Mac's rejection. Better to wonder what might be than to know that he thought of her as just a business partner or worse, a child. Better to . . .

No, she told herself. Don't run away again. Hadn't she learned anything from her time in the business? She was a strong, capable woman. She had things to offer a man. Mac would be a fool to turn her down. She ought to march right over and demand that they discuss their feelings for each other.

"How long are you going to stand there staring at my back?" he asked without turning around.

Her mind went blank and she drew in a ragged breath. "Not much longer."

"Are you ready to go home?"

"Yes."

He rose quickly, dusting the sand from his tailored slacks. Despite his preference for casual clothing, he always dressed up when visiting his father. Lynn insisted on formality, even among family members.

See, Amy wanted to tell her mother. He abides by your wishes, even when he has no reason to. He's not the black sheep; he's not irresponsible. He's just a man making his own way in the world.

The elegant attire concealed his tanned skin, but not the bulk of the muscles tightly coiled beneath. She wasn't sure if she liked him better dressed up or down. Perhaps her favorite would be not dressed at all.

Mac held out his hand. Placing her palm in his, she savored the sensation of their fingers lacing together. The transfer of heat threatened to engulf her in flames. Now, she told herself. This is the time to speak with him . . . to admit how confused she was about her feelings, to ask him about his.

"Ah, kid, I guess it's just you and me again." He ruffled her bangs and pulled her toward the walkway. "I'll let you off bait detail on the next fishing trip, if we don't have to go back inside and say good-bye."

She tried to smile, but her mouth was strangely stiff. Kid? He'd called her kid? "Sure, Mac. No problem. I told my mom we were leaving as soon as I found you."

"Good."

They walked silently to the motorcycle. Amy hadn't allowed herself to cry since she'd miscarried the baby. Even tonight at dinner, when Mac had been hurt by his father, she'd been able to fight back the tears. But now, as the tall, dark man at her side paused to carefully set the crash helmet on her head, she felt the moisture welling up behind her lids.

It was worse than losing him; she'd never even been in the running. The issue of loving or not loving didn't matter. Just like the first time they'd met, she thought. Nothing had changed since she was sixteen.

He swung one long leg over the powerful machine. She followed suit. As the engine flared to life, she wrapped her arms around his back and pressed her face into the smooth cotton of his shirt.

What now? Did she give up? Did she fight for something she wasn't sure she could handle? Did she move to Antarctica? Did she show up naked in his room and hope he'd get the message?

The picture of a very shocked Mac Spirno pulling up the sheet to cover himself and issuing pleas to defend his honor made her giggle. Still, the question remained. What now?

Mac eased the machine into gear and started down the driveway. Amy's soft body pressed against him like a loving cape of hot satin. Twin points burned into his back, while her arms wrapped around his waist, her hands clutching him just above the button of his trousers.

Good thing their positions weren't reversed, he thought as they drove through the night. Then she'd know exactly how much he wanted her. Even now it was difficult not to push her fingers down those last few inches and allow her to caress the ridge of his desire.

They moved swiftly through the warm night air. The sound of the ocean was lost in the traffic and the thundering of his heart. He wanted her and there wasn't a damned thing he was going to do about it.

His father's words came back to haunt him. The idea of a wife and a family certainly had its own appeal and yet . . . How could he ask any woman to commit to a relationship when he wasn't convinced he had what it took to make one work? He was good in a clinch, romantic and otherwise, but what about over the long haul? There had been a lot of years of doing what he wanted, with no one to answer to. Could he be there in sickness and in health, or would he cut out at the first sign of trouble?

He'd only loved one thing in his life and that was the sea. Everything else had come and gone with a minimum of feeling on his part. Would it be the same with a woman?

Mac tried to imagine life without Amy. But it was impossible to picture the house empty of her presence or the office back to its old chaos. She had changed his world. Was there enough between them to change him?

He turned the motorcycle into the long drive and slowed to a stop in front of the house. She slipped off the back and removed her helmet.

"Want some coffee?" she asked, smoothing down her blonde hair.

"No. I think I'll drive around a little more." He shifted into first. "Don't wait up."

"Mac, I . . ." Disappointment flared in her eyes. The firm set of her mouth trembled.

If he could hurt her without even trying, what would he be capable of in the heat of anger? "Night, Amy."

He rode past the city and on down to the Keys. The miles of land and bridges slipped under the rapidly spinning tires of his bike. When he couldn't go any farther, he parked the motorcycle and walked to the edge of the water.

Sitting alone, he waited for the sun to break the darkness. If he was any kind of man, he'd fight for Amy and what they could have together. He'd been raised on cowboys and soldiers in those great old movies. Heroes who fought, no matter the odds, no matter the cost. But he wasn't a storybook character and there was no guarantee of a happy ending. He was just a man trying to make things come out right. He'd spent his whole life doing what he wanted to do. Maybe it was time to put someone else first.

Easy enough in theory, he thought as the first glimmer of light rippled across the sea. But how was he to know what was best for Amy?

The Coast Guard Auxiliary boating skills' class was held in a school, next to the military grounds. Amy clutched her notebook close to her chest as she walked beside Mac.

"I haven't had math in a long time," she said cautiously, glancing at the large armada of ships tied up at the slips.

"No one's going to test you on logarithms. There's a little meteorology, some chart reading, and coastal navigation. You'll do fine."

"Uh-huh." She didn't look convinced. "With my luck, the room will be filled with experienced sailors, and they'll find out right away that I don't know a thing."

Mac grinned and held open the door to the classroom. "I'm sure you'll muddle through."

But his grin died when he stepped into the room. Ten young uniformed officers stood talking with each other. All conversation ceased when Amy walked to the front of the class and spoke with the man at the podium. He could feel them studying every inch of her leggy body, from the tip of her blonde head, past the skimpy T-shirt and shorts, down to her sandal-clad feet. They all looked so young, he thought grimly. And tall. No doubt she'd swoon at the sight of the freshly-pressed uniforms.

An unfamiliar emotion uncoiled in his belly, sending white-hot anger to every nerve ending. Why the hell had he insisted she take this class? So what if she needed it for her captain's license? Maybe it was also offered at the local senior citizen home.

Amy thanked the man in charge and returned to Mac's side. "This is the place," she said, smiling with confidence. "Several officers are going to sit in on the class.

It's part of their training to be instructors. Isn't that great?''

Mac glanced at the pack of men waiting to tear sweet Amy apart. He could feel them moving closer, mentally rehearsing their opening lines. He was ready to punch out the first one who asked her what her sign was. ''Yeah.''

She glanced at her watch. ''It's almost time. You can leave now. I'll be fine.''

Mac looked desperately around the room. The rest of the class seemed to be made up of young kids and retired men. The only other woman was about sixty-five. ''Maybe I should stay with you and, ah, help with the note taking. You haven't been in school in a long time.''

''Mac, please.'' She gave him a gentle shove toward the door. ''I'm not a five-year-old entering kindergarten for the first time. I'll be fine. Now, get out of here.''

He cast one more warning glare toward the rapidly approaching pack, but they didn't even slow down. ''I'll be back in two hours,'' he said when he reached the hall. ''Be careful.''

When he returned to pick her up, she was standing in the center of a group of men, talking away. Mac fought the urge to assume an offensive position and start swinging. He knew better than to think he could take on ten trained military men at once. Besides, what if Amy liked one of them? He wouldn't want to stand in her way.

Yet the sight of one of the men casually resting his hand on her arm made him want to spill some blood. Shouldering his way through the crowd, he stopped next to her.

"How did it go?" he growled.

"Mac! Hi. Guys, this is my partner, Mac."

The men shook hands. He wanted to grab her and run, but she seemed quite content to keep them chatting. "We've been invited to tour one of the ships," she said, smiling up at him.

"Swell."

Suddenly, she stepped closer and slipped her arm around his waist. "Another time, gentlemen. We've got a fishing charter to get ready for." Her blue eyes met his and he had the sneaking suspicion she saw too damned much.

As they walked to the car, she giggled.

"What's so funny?" he asked.

"Men."

"All men, or one or two in particular?"

She reached up and kissed his cheek. "You, in particular, Mac. Just you."

Mac hated institutions. They were a necessary part of life, but he avoided them whenever possible. That was the main reason he hadn't wanted to be a lawyer. The thought of spending his day locked up with briefs and old books was enough to send him screaming from the room. Even now, as he crossed the lobby of the old bank building, he could feel the walls closing in on him.

His appointment was at ten. As he slid into the chair opposite the loan officer's desk, the old clock began to chime the hour.

"Right on time, Napoleon. Your father would be pleased."

Mac grinned. "Cut to the chase, Harry. I want some

money. I've got a gun in my coat and I'm not afraid to take you with me."

The older gray-haired man frowned. His half-glasses slipped further down his nose and made him look like a studious turtle. "I've told you, we don't appreciate hold-up humor here at First National."

Harry Simpson was the senior loan officer at the bank and an old friend of the family. He and Mac's father had gone to high school together, dated and lost the same girls. But instead of attending a prestigious college, Harry had decided to see the world. He'd never made it as far on the road to success, but Mac felt he'd lived the more fulfilling life. It was hard not to like a man who spent his weekends fishing off a dock and making friends with the local seagulls.

Mac leaned back in his chair and grinned. "Okay. How about a loan, then."

"For what? Another one of your fancy boats?"

He sighed. "No. To buy out my partner."

The old man whistled silently. "Based on your last financial statement, that's going to be a big loan. I'm not sure you'll qualify."

"I have to."

"The partnership isn't working out?"

Mac pictured Amy's laughing face. His gut tightened as he remembered the passion he'd felt in her kiss, the way she watched him with that mixture of longing and confusion in her eyes. He'd never been noble before in his life, but by God, he was going to be noble enough to let her go.

"No, it's not."

Harry shuffled the papers on his desk. "Would you need a lump sum, or could it be done with payments?"

"I think she'd agree to payments."

Harry nodded. "Let me see what I can do. We might have to mortgage the house for this."

"Whatever it takes is fine with me, just as long as by the time the six months are up, Amy is free to walk away."

NINE

"The rabbit goes around the hole and under the tree."

Bob rolled his eyes. "Amy, a rabbit can't go under a tree. Here." He took the length of rope from her hands and demonstrated the knot again. "The rabbit goes around the tree and back in the hole."

She leaned against the storage compartment and laughed. "Do I look like a person who cares?"

They were sitting on the dock, waiting for the last charter of the day to return. Amy glanced at the lime green zinc oxide on Bob's nose and wondered if she looked as foolish.

It was almost the end of June and the weather had turned muggy. Her tank top clung to her in sweaty patches. "I would kill for a glass of ice water."

There were footsteps behind them, then a cold drop fell on her arm and she glanced up. Mac held a can of soda tantalizingly out of reach. "I'd settle for you being my love slave."

His laughing eyes held her captive and she all but forgot the interested observer at her side. "Sold," she said, stretching up for the drink. "When do I report for duty?"

Mac grinned and tossed Bob a second can. "We'll discuss that later. What are you two doing down here."

"Waiting for Mary and trying to learn knots. I hate all this rabbit stuff."

Bob chuckled. "Yeah. She keeps wanting to send the rabbit under the tree."

"Ahoy! Permission to dock!"

Mac shaded his eyes and stared out into the marina. "Freddy? Is that you? I didn't think you were still alive, you ancient sea dog. Come on alongside."

Amy and Bob stood up as a beautiful old sailboat eased in next to the end slip. The wooden hull gleamed with varnish and attention. White sails billowed and snapped in the late afternoon breeze. The man at the wheel was old, probably close to eighty, with the dark, leathered face of someone who'd spent his life at sea. A cap was pulled down over gray hair and a cracked pipe stuck out from one side of his mouth.

Amy stood on tiptoe and peered into the cockpit, half expecting to see a one-eyed dog sitting at his feet.

When the craft was a couple of feet from the dock, Bob grabbed the line and tied her fast. Mac grinned and moved to the end of the slip. "Permission to come on board, captain."

"Permission granted. How are you, Mac? Still carting them rich folks around the marina? Aren't you ready to earn your living like a real man?"

Mac chuckled and pulled Freddy into a bear hug. "Nothing in the world could make me get up at two in the morning." He turned to Amy and motioned for her to join him. "This old grouch is always trying to convince me to be a fisherman."

"Nothin' like it." Freddy winked at Amy. "What's a pretty thing like you doing with a scoundrel like this boy?" He gave her a courtly bow, then indicated everyone should sit on the bench behind the steering wheel.

Mac slipped his arm around her shoulders. "She's the woman Nappy left half the business to."

"You don't say." Freddy's pale blue eyes looked as though the sun had bleached away most of the color, but Amy had the feeling nothing got by the old man. "What do you think of all this?" His wide-open gesture took in the docks and boats, along with the ocean.

She smiled. "I'm learning slowly. It's fun. I like it."

"In my day, women were considered bad luck on a ship. Always thought that silly superstition was invented by men who sailed to get away from their wives."

"Freddy used to fish the northern coast. He was also in the Navy during the Second World War," Mac said.

"Really?" Amy was impressed. "I'd love to hear your stories."

"I'd be happy to oblige. In fact, when I know you a little better, I might even show you one of my favorite scars."

Mac groaned. "Don't get him started. He can talk for days."

Freddy pulled a flask out of his shirt pocket and took a swig. "Lies. All lies. The boy's jealous of my way with the ladies."

Amy leaned forward and patted the old man's arm. "He has reason to be."

"I like this one," Freddy said. "You'd do well to keep her around."

"Enough flattery, from both of you," Mac said. "What brings you here?"

Freddy sighed. "My youngest daughter wants me to live with her in San Diego. Hard to believe, I know, but I'm getting on in years. It's lonely, sometimes, with all the boys gone." He looked over Amy's left shoulder, seeing a past she couldn't begin to imagine. "Mac, you've been after me for years about this boat. I'm putting her up for sale and thought I'd give you first shot."

Mac rose to his feet and walked toward the cabin. Amy read the indecision in his step. He wanted the boat. She could see it in the way he ran his hands lovingly over the transom, as though caressing a very special woman. Deep inside, a shudder started as she wondered what it would feel like to have those fingers touching her so tenderly.

He turned back, regret darkening his eyes and pulling his mouth into a straight line. "Thanks, Freddy, but I can't. All my money is tied up in the bank and they won't give me another loan."

"I'll give you the money," Amy offered without thinking.

"You don't make enough. I know, I've seen your paycheck."

"I have some from my trust. When my father died, there was a small insurance policy. Mother gave me the funds when I turned twenty-one. They're just sitting in an account."

Hope flared, then died. "We're talking about a hundred thousand dollars."

She did a quick calculation. "I have that." Of course, that was all she had, but she'd gladly loan it to Mac.

He shook his head. "Sorry, Freddy. Another time. I'm sure you'll be able to find a buyer for this beauty."

The old man shrugged. "Ain't much call for wooden boats these days, even with all them new fangled gadgets I put in. Folks are more interested in new than quality."

"All you need is one enthusiast," Mac said. "Thanks for thinking of me."

Amy wanted to stomp her foot in frustration. Why wouldn't Mac let her help? Was it male pride or did the resistance go deeper? Maybe he was keeping their lives separate so that when the six months were over, he could walk away without looking back.

Amy checked her heading on the compass and pushed the rudder a little more to starboard. In another half hour or so, Mary's fishing charter should be in sight. Casting a critical eye at her sails, she made a small adjustment to the jib, tightening it in the growing breeze. She'd love to get back early and shock Mac.

This was her test. She was to sail out to Mary's boat, retrieve a sealed letter, and return it to Mac. The task would prove her ability to sail, navigate, and find a specific location—and whether or not she had her sea legs. A small radio sat in the cockpit of the thirty-two-foot craft, but she'd promised herself she wouldn't use it. In the last few months, ever since she'd asked to become a part of the business, she'd been training for this moment. She knew she could do it; confidence filled her with quiet satisfaction.

It was just a matter of putting in enough hours at sea and then she could apply for her six-pack license. That would allow her to take up to six passengers on day fishing trips. Over the next couple of years, she'd move up until, finally, she was licensed to captain the *Christina*.

Plans, some more formed than others, flitted through her mind. There were so many ways she could help the business grow. Some of her ideas were contained in her computer, the calculations almost complete, others needed a little more time and confidence until she presented them to her often-confusing partner.

Amy tucked a stray strand of hair under her baseball cap and took a drink from the thermos. How was she supposed to convince Mac that she was all grown up? Ever since her mother had said that magic sentence, she'd had a hard time thinking of anything else. The issue of loving Mac still remained a mystery, but she knew that she wanted him.

Not a day went by that she didn't find herself weak with longing. Every night she listened for his movements in the house. It was getting more and more difficult to avoid going to his room and pleading with him to take her.

Damn it, this was the nineties! She could do that if she wanted to.

A seagull swooped down close to the boat. Its squawking chatter seemed to dare her to action. "All right," she said aloud. "I will. Tonight."

She paused, waiting for the sinking feeling of fear that would surely pool in her stomach. Instead, there was a flash of trepidation, followed by satisfaction. One way or the other, she'd find out where she stood.

Taking a deep breath, she tried to ignore the liquid heat warming the blood in her veins. The desire she felt had never been in question. But did she *love* him?

In her mind's eye, she could see the concern in his face when she'd been seasick. Her body remembered the way he'd carried her to the car and fussed over her like a worried mother hen. He'd been there for her when she'd married and again in the hospital after she'd lost the baby. Even when she'd demanded to encroach on his exclusive territory in the business, he'd been willing to see her side of the issue and allow her to be a full partner. He was a good man. Better than any she'd ever known.

A faint noise caught her attention. Squinting against the sunlight, she saw a bobbing white boat in the distance. Mary! She'd done it!

Within a few minutes, she'd pulled alongside the sports fisherman and boarded.

"Welcome the conquering hero," Mary said, her tanned face creased with a grin. "I knew you could do it, Amy. Congratulations."

"Don't celebrate my victory prematurely. I still have to make it back to shore."

"You will. That's the easy part. All you have to do is hit Florida, then follow the coast to the marina."

The five fishermen glanced at them quizzically, but stayed on the alert at their fishing poles. Amy grinned. "I'd better head back. I want to surprise Mac by being early."

Mary gave her a quick hug. "Here's the letter." She handed over a sealed envelope. "Give it to Mac as proof that you made it. Good luck, Amy. See you back at the dock."

Amy climbed back into the sailboat and cast off. The wind picked up, moving her craft swiftly across the water. After folding the letter in half, she tucked it into her shorts' pocket. She'd done it! The victory was sweet.

Mac paced restlessly on the dock. Raising the binoculars to his eyes, he peered out over the ocean. Nothing. Not a single hint of a sail in the distance. Where the hell was she?

"Yo! Bossman!" Bob strolled up beside him. "Amy's not due back for another two hours. You'll make yourself bonkers waiting out here. You should get away for awhile, man."

Mac glanced at his employee. "I know. I can't help worrying, though. What if something happens to her?"

"She's got the radio. She'll call for help if she needs it. Besides . . ." He swept out his arm. "It's a beautiful day. Good wind, clear weather. Mary radioed to say Amy was on her way back." He patted Mac on the back. "She'll be fine."

"Thanks. You're right. If I can distract myself, the time will go faster. I have that boat to look over." He abandoned his post at the dock and started toward the workshop. Halfway down the ramp, he paused and looked out to sea. *Come back to me, Amy*, he pleaded silently.

The oil leak turned out to be worse than he'd thought. After finding and fixing the cause, he decided that he might as well go over the rest of the engine. When he'd done all he could, he stuck a hose in the water intake valve and turned on the tap. As liquid gushed over the machinery, he started the engine.

It grumbled a bit, then roared into life. Not bad, Spirno, he thought, wiping his hands on a clean cloth. If he ever got tired of the ocean, he could always get a job at a gas station.

He glanced at the clock and noted the time, then shut off the engine and strolled over to the sink to clean up. The rich lather was up around his elbows when he realized how late it was. Panic and concern flooded him, washing away every thought but one: Where was Amy? If anything had happened to her, he'd never be able to live with himself.

Barely pausing to rinse, he raced to the door of the building and jerked it open. "Bob, have you heard . . ."

"Hi, Mac." Amy stood halfway down the ramp. Her blue eyes sparkled with excitement and success. "I thought you'd be waiting for me, but I guess you knew there wouldn't be a problem."

He stared at her hungrily, taking in her delicate features before dropping his gaze to the fullness of her breasts pressing against the soft cotton of her T-shirt. He'd never allowed himself to think she might have an accident at sea, but that hadn't taken away the niggling sense of fear eating away at his soul.

She was beautiful . . . she was alive . . . she was here.

"Amy." Moving forward swiftly, he caught her in his arms and pulled her against him. Her feet dangled off the ground as he swung her around. "You made it back. That's my girl."

He buried his face in the curve of her neck and inhaled the scent of her perfume and the sea. Her combination of lean lines and gentle curves threatened his rapidly unwinding cords of self-control. The vibration of her laughter was transferred from her chest to his; the movement started a deeper rumbling that had nothing to do with amusement.

She put her baseball cap on his head and tugged it over his forehead, then let her fingers linger on his hair and shoulders. "I have a letter for you from Mary."

He let her slide to the ground, the length of her body slipping against his in erotic punishment. "You read it."

Amy had to force herself to look away from Mac's warm gaze. His eyes seemed to be caressing her with an almost physical sensation. Tremors began deep inside, slowly working their way to the surface. By the time she'd pulled the sealed envelope from her pocket, she could feel her heart pounding foolishly against her chest.

His pleasure at her success didn't mean anything, she told herself firmly. He would have been just as happy if it had been Bob. A grin tugged at her lips as she tried to imagine the two men allowing themselves to hug each other. Not in this lifetime, she thought.

After tearing open the envelope, she unfolded the letter. "I never had any doubt in your ability," she read aloud. "I'm proud of you and so is Nappy. Love, Mac." She turned to the man in question. "You wrote this before I left."

He nodded. "Gave it to Mary when she took off this morning." His smile faded as he leaned closer. "Are those tears in your eyes? Don't cry, Amy. I thought you'd be pleased."

"I am," she whispered, moved by his faith. "And I'm not crying. It's just . . ."

She wrapped her arms around his waist and held him close. "Thank you, Mac. For everything."

"I didn't do a thing."

"Yes, you did. You believed in me. Even when I wasn't sure I believed in myself." Her hands crept up his arms to rest on his broad shoulders. In a heartbeat, awareness replaced gratitude.

His eyes met hers, the dark brown deepening to black. A spark flared for a moment, then he blinked and it was lost. But she was sure she'd seen the flash.

They were alone at the far end of the dock. All the boats were in but one, and it wasn't due for another hour. Bob had left on an errand and the office was empty. In fact, the entire world had disappeared, leaving just her and Mac and the tangible need growing between them.

"Mac," she whispered, swaying lightly in his arms.

"Amy, don't ask me this. I'm doing my damnedest to keep my promise and stay away."

She licked her lower lip quickly, then paused and slowly repeated the act when she saw he was mesmerized by the action. "I'm not asking," she said, pressing her hips against his. "And I'm not interested in your promise. I want you. It's time. We both know that."

He hesitated as though he were going to disagree, then offered a low groan of agreement and bent down to claim her lips. Their first kiss, twelve years before, had taught as much as it had excited. Her youth and innocence had prevented any chance of further exploration. Their second kiss, in the quiet of her bedroom after the disastrous sail, had been a discovery of sorts, relearning the parameters of sensation, defining the boundaries of their pleasure. A common element in both contacts had been control. At no time had she felt Mac was acting with a force that threatened to sweep them both away.

This time, when his mouth descended upon hers, she felt consumed. His lips pressed against hers, absorbing then reflecting the intolerable heat burning through her body.

Everything was hard. The muscles of his shoulders tensed until she felt she were kneading living, breathing stone. His mouth was all firm need, moving from side to side, leaving no part of her sensitized flesh uncaressed. Long legs nestled intimately with hers until she felt the light tickling of the dark hair and the corded strength beneath. One large hand moved her hips back and forth, rubbing her stomach over the erection pressing against his shorts.

His tongue plunged inside her mouth. The second they touched, she felt the fire race down to her toes and back, settling into an inferno between her thighs.

As they reached and tasted, circling endlessly, moving in and out, mocking the motion their bodies ached to perform, she knew there was no going back. Somehow, they had crossed the line and he was hers.

Moving her hands down his chest, she savored her victory. For once, his regulation T-shirt had been replaced by the buttoned variety. She started at the bottom, ripping off one button in her haste.

Mac chuckled, then raised his head and cupped her jaw in his hands. His thumbs touched her nose, then swept across her cheeks, while his fingers played with her ears. "I hardly think this is the place."

"What?" She looked around and saw they were still

standing in front of the boathouse. "Oh my. I didn't realize . . ." A blush crept up her neck and face.

"Yeah. Me, too." His voice was husky with passion, his eyes glazed with desire. "I suggest we continue this conversation at the house."

Together, they raced up the ramp to the office. After locking the doors, they turned toward the parking lot. Amy's car sat beside the motorcycle.

Mac glanced from one vehicle to the other. "There's no way in hell I'm letting you out of my sight." He jogged back to the office, then quickly returned with an extra crash helmet. "Put this on."

He swung a leg over the bike and started the engine. Amy fumbled with the chin strap, her fingers trembling with need. When she'd accomplished her task, she slid behind him, pressing her body as close to his as possible.

The vibration from the machine rumbled deliciously through her already aroused core. The urge to pull off her shirt and bra and rest her bare breasts against Mac's back was strong, but she resisted. Being arrested for indecent exposure wasn't part of her plan for the evening. It was only a few miles to the house. Surely, she could hold on till then.

Starting at his left shoulder and moving slowly to the right, she nibbled. Some bites were gentle reminders of her presence, some were deeper, frustrated messages to get them there *quickly*.

At the end of the highway off-ramp, she slipped her hands under his shirt and began a teasing ascent to the center of his chest. The hairs parted beneath her fingers. She could feel the thundering beat of his heart, hear the rapid cadence of her breath, taste the anticipation of what would be.

At a stoplight, he glanced over his shoulder. "You're driving me crazy."

She rubbed her breasts lightly against his back. "I know."

"Don't stop."

When he pulled in front of the house, she didn't step off the machine. Instead, she continued to touch his chest. From shoulder to waist, she massaged every inch, danced over every rib. When she couldn't bear the hairs rubbing over her sensitized palms, she paused, her fingers resting on the snap of his shorts.

One large hand cupped hers, then moved it over the ridge of his desire. She felt the hardness press against her palm and she squeezed lightly. A shudder raced through his body.

Moving in tandem, they left the bike and walked quickly to the door. While Amy removed her helmet, Mac fumbled with the key. When she slammed the door behind them, he undid his own strap and dropped his helmet on the floor.

Desire etched harsh lines in his face. She swallowed against the tightness in her throat. The need to be next to him, to take him inside of her until there were no limits to him and her, only the ultimate closeness of mating, made her legs tremble and threaten to give way.

"Mac," she whispered urgently, trying to express with that single word all the explosive feelings in her heart.

With one fluid movement, he bent down and swept her into his arms. Long strides carried her to his bedroom at the far end of the house. She'd been in his arms before, but never like this.

When he set her in front of the bed, she clung to him for support. Without warning, his mouth claimed hers once again. Tongues pushed their way forward, ignoring the niceties observed before. The dance took on a frantic edge. There was no time to be polite, there was only white-hot need.

His hands were everywhere. Calloused palms rubbed against her stomach as he lifted the T-shirt up and over her head. Her breasts ached in eager anticipation, but he moved on quickly, removing his own shirt, then dropping his shorts. Deck shoes joined the rapidly growing pile. And still they kissed.

She sucked on his lower lip, then bit and sucked again. His lean fingers traced spirals up and down her side and ribs, inching closer to her lace-clad breasts, but never quite touching. Only when he unhooked the front catch did his knuckles brush the curves.

As the bra whispered to the floor, she felt her nipples swell and harden in the air. Touch them, she pleaded silently. But his hands were intent on removing the triangle of lace on her hips. It joined its mate and was then covered by white briefs.

Once again, she was caught up in his arms. The journey was far too short for her to absorb the feeling of crisp chest hairs against her breasts. In a matter of seconds, she was lowered on the bed. The spread was soft and cool against her heated skin.

Mac knelt above her. The lazy male smile promised a thousand delights. "I want you," he murmured.

Her eyes dropped lower, taking in the broad chest,

then drifting down to the proof of his desire. Her hand tiptoed across his knee, then slightly higher to his thigh.

He stiffened visibly, then swooped down and claimed her mouth. Moist heat plunged in and out of her lips, while magical fingers moved closer and closer to her breasts. She arched her back, indicating her need. At last, he touched the full bottom curve. She gasped her delight.

With maddening slowness, he learned every millimeter of creamy skin, spiraling higher and higher, circling her nipples but never quite touching. Her hips rotated in silent supplication. Their legs tangled and she felt his erection seeking against her thigh. Her hands touched his back and buttocks, urging him on further.

At last his mouth began to trail kisses down her neck and throat. He hadn't shaved that morning and his stubble grated erotically, arousing the skin it caressed. At last his tongue approached a turgid peak and he paused.

Their eyes met. Fire flared. When she was sure she would explode, he took the nipple in his mouth and tasted the puckered nub. The sensation of hot moisture caressing her was almost more than she could bear. First, the broad width of his tongue bathed the rosy point with lingering attention, then the tip dueled until she moaned her surrender.

The other breast ached, awaiting its turn in paradise. At last, he shifted his head and the other was assuaged. His nimble fingers imitated the action of his tongue and she felt the fire roaring down her belly. Liquid need poured into her, readying her for his final assault.

But first he meant to kill her with attention. Long, slow, wet kisses trailed past her navel and between her legs. His face rubbed against her thighs as his tongue sought and pleasured her damp core.

Weeks before she had wondered about his claim to patience. When the sheets grew tangled and the wanting irresistible, did he still draw upon a bottomless well?

Yes, she thought as a gasp escaped her parted lips. Oh, yes. How slowly he tortured her, with endless circles and well-timed licks. When she tensed to urge him to go faster, he slowed even more. Each movement became a dance of pleasure, choreographed with need and sweat-slicked passion.

Embers sparked, then grew, fed by her deepening sighs. Flames engulfed her as she tossed her head from side to side, unable to do more than draw breath after breath. Her hands clutched at the spread, squeezing the fabric. Her hips lifted higher and higher, as if to retain forever the glory of his loving. When his hands gripped her buttocks and urged her, she felt the dynamite of the explosion that tore her body apart.

He caught her as she fell. In the aftermath, as the tremors threatened to leave her forever broken, his strong arms held her tightly against his chest. His scent was her beacon, his steady heartbeat her shelter.

She opened her eyes, then blinked to bring everything back in focus. "M—Mac?"

"Hush," he said softly. "Don't say anything."

Ripples of pleasure lingered, causing her leg to jerk slightly as she rested safe in her haven. He had taken her to a place she hadn't been sure existed. Emotions threatened to overwhelm her, but she pushed them aside. For tonight, there was only this man. He was her world. All else was insubstantial.

Mac held her loosely in his arms, careful to keep

his touch light. The flush of her release was only now beginning to drain away. The throbbing between his legs demanded attention, but he willed it to be quiet for now. It was enough to savor her reaction and trust.

Her blue eyes were serious, but relaxed, under half-closed lids. Her lips were red and swollen from his kisses. He wanted her.

One of her hands toyed with his hair, the other traced lazy patterns on his chest. He felt the exact moment the contact changed from slow and sated to aroused.

Scooting lower on the bed, she parted her mouth and urged him to sup his full. Nails raked lightly across his back, then moved around to toy with his hardness. A groan centered itself in his chest. How could one sweet woman contain so much passion, he wondered, as she threatened to push him over the edge.

As he knelt between her thighs, she opened for him. Protection was reached for and used, then he pushed forward, pausing when he encountered her wet tightness. There'd be no more play tonight, he thought as he eased inside. She stretched to accommodate his length, then wrapped her legs around his hips.

Her sweet smile urged him onward, while her rapid reactions to his thrusts made her impossible to resist. Next time, he promised himself as the sensation built. Pressure grew until he was ready to drown in the need. At last, when his harsh breathing filled the silence of the room, he broke through to the surface, groaning out his release.

Amy stirred against the heavy warmth resting on her back. Her first thought was that she'd left her electric blanket on high. Her second was that she didn't own an electric blanket. Her third was that no blanket, electric or not, had ever played with her breasts.

She opened her eyes and watched Mac's hand tease her responsive flesh into arousal.

"Morning," she murmured, her voice still thick with sleep.

"Good morning, yourself. How do you feel?"

She stretched against him, reveling in the tangling of legs and brushing of arms, then smiled when she felt the ache in her thighs. "Mmm. A little stiff, but very satisfied." She rolled to face him and reached a finger up to trace his jaw.

He shrugged, half proud, half guilty. "Me, too. But I shouldn't have been so enthusiastic when we made love after dinner."

"I think the real damage was done . . ." She leaned over his shoulder and looked at the clock. The digital numbers showed the time to be after nine in the morning. ". . . about three hours ago. I'd always heard that men woke up aroused, but I confess I've never experienced it so fully before."

He kissed her neck. "I aim to please."

She pushed at his chest until he was resting on his back, then leaned over and touched his lips. "You do . . . very well."

"Such beauty." His hands smoothed her hair, then shifted her weight until she straddled him. "As I've said before, you're an amazing woman, princess." He grimaced. "Sorry."

"I think after last night, you can call me anything you'd like."

His smile turned into a moan as she shifted slightly and eased him inside her.

"We probably shouldn't do this again so soon," he said, not sounding too convincing.

"Probably not," she agreed, bending over and brushing his lips with hers. "In fact—"

"Amy?"

"Yes?"

His hands clasped her hips and moved her back and forth.

"Can we finish this conversation later?"

She smiled and tightened her muscles. "Absolutely."

TEN

"It's only three days," Amy offered.

"I know." Mac looked as disappointed as a kid being told his little league game was rained out. "But I wish I could send someone else."

"You can't. As you love to point out to me everyday—you're the captain here. You said you'd take the *Christina* and you have to do it. These corporate types need to be dazzled, and you're good at that. I'll be fine."

He leaned over her desk and hungrily kissed her lips. The brief contact sent fire sizzling through her blood.

"It's not you I'm worried about," he murmured against her mouth. "It's me. How will I survive three nights alone?"

Amy stood and stretched. "I don't know about you, but I'm looking forward to sleeping the whole night through."

Guilt flashed in his eyes. "Have I been keeping you up too much?"

She moved next to him and slid her hands up his chest. "If I remember correctly, I'm the one who beat the alarm this morning."

"Yes." He nibbled her neck. "You were quite insistent. Even demanding."

"Will it always . . . be like this. Ah!" She arched toward him as his fingers toyed with her breasts.

Mac looked at her, his dark eyes suddenly serious. "Amy, I . . ."

The office door opened. "Geez, you two should get a sign or something. This is worse than having teenagers in the house." Mary tapped her foot impatiently and grinned. "Should I come back?"

"No. Of course not. Mac was just leaving." She pushed him toward the door.

"I was?" he asked.

"Yes. I'll meet you on board the *Amata* in the Keys in three days."

He gave her a quick kiss. "I'll count the hours. Don't be late."

She watched him walk toward the dock, then called after him. "Don't forget, you promised I get to captain the trip."

He put his hands over his ears. "I can't hear you."

"Good-bye." She waited until he'd boarded the cabin cruiser, then turned back to her employee. "What can I do for you, Mary?"

"I need these invoices okayed."

The older woman handed her the papers, then plopped down on the cracked vinyl sofa and eyed her speculatively. "So, you're going to try the trip up from the Keys again?"

Amy nodded. "Yup." She touched her stomach.

"Hopefully, I'll have a better showing this time." It was a repeat of the first sailing trip she'd taken with Mac . . . the one that had ended in disaster.

After totaling the invoices, she checked the bottom line with the quotes she'd received, then initialed the corner. "Looks great. How's the varnishing going?"

Mary grinned. "Bob's still a little miffed, but I think the company's doing a great job. I'd pay them twice this amount to never touch another piece of sandpaper as long as I live."

Amy leaned back in her chair. "I know Mac would rather be drawn and quartered than admit someone else might do as good a job as he would, but even he mentioned their work didn't stink!"

The two women laughed together.

Mary glanced around the room, then out the window. "You serious about all this?" Her hand indicated the room, but Amy knew she meant her relationship with Mac.

"Yes. I think so. It's all very new and exciting, but I believe we have a good shot at making things work out."

Mary smiled. "I'm happy for both of you. Mac has needed to settle down for a long time and I think you're strong enough to keep him in line."

"He is stubborn, isn't he?"

"And opinionated." Mary walked toward the door. "But he has a great butt."

Their eyes met. "I couldn't agree more."

Amy picked up the phone and tucked it between her ear and her shoulder. "Spirno Marine. May I help you?"

"Amy! My dear, how are you?"

"Fine, Mom. What's up?"

"Oh, Amy. I just wanted to say how sorry I was. I want you to know that you're welcome to stay at the house for as long as you need to. And that job managing the boutique is still open, if you're interested."

"Hold on a minute." Amy saved her spreadsheet and turned away from the computer. A cold knot was forming in the pit of her stomach, but she tried to ignore the sensation. "I don't understand what you're talking about. I have a job and a place to stay."

"Mac hasn't told you then?" Her mother's voice was warm and filled with maternal concern. That frightened her more than any words.

"T–told me what."

"I don't think that I should be the one to—"

"Mom, if you have some information that affects me, I'd like to know."

"Oh, Amy." Lynn sighed heavily. "A friend of the judge's is a loan officer at First National. Last night at dinner he mentioned Mac had applied for a loan. He thought we knew all about it and I didn't tell him otherwise."

The cold feeling had spread to the rest of her body, making her limbs seem leaden and her breathing slow and difficult. She almost knew what was coming, but she had to hear the words all the same. "What did Mac want a loan for?"

"I'm so sorry, dear. After our last talk I've been thinking about what you said. I never meant to make you wonder if I love you. Of course, I do. You're my child. I wouldn't hurt you for the world."

Despite the comforting phrases, she could still feel

the approaching pain. "I appreciate that. Really. I realize things have changed for us. Now, tell me about the loan."

"Mac wants to buy you out."

"What? Why?"

"I don't know."

She clutched the phone and tried to catch her breath. The tightening pressure in her chest made it difficult to breath.

"Amy? Amy, are you still there?"

"Yes, Mom." She spoke softly, each word forced out past stiff, frozen lips.

"I'm sorry, honey. You worked hard to make the partnership successful. For what it's worth, I think you did a fine job with the company and . . ." She sighed. "I'm sorry he hurt you. If there's anything I can do . . ."

"I know. Thanks."

Amy didn't remember saying good-bye. She didn't remember hanging up the phone. The next thing she knew, she was standing at the window and staring out over the ocean. Despite the hot, muggy Florida day, she wondered if she'd ever be warm again. Even her heart felt as though it had been encased in ice.

Why? she asked silently. She wasn't sure which was worse: that he wanted her out of the partnership or that he'd gone to get the loan without telling her. Didn't he appreciate all that she'd done for the business? Didn't their months together mean anything? Didn't he care that she loved him?

Her breath caught in her throat, then escaped with a sigh. Dear God, she loved him. Looking back, she realized she always had. The crush from her schoolgirl days had simply matured into adult love. There'd never been a time when Mac Spirno hadn't been the center of her universe. And now, he was throwing everything away.

She glanced at her watch and swore. Her assistant wasn't due in for another three hours. Still, there was time. She could get back to the house, pack, and be gone long before Mac returned. Her mother would help her. Maybe this time she'd go to Dallas or Chicago. She never wanted to see the ocean again. She never wanted to feel the warmth of the sun on her skin, taste the saltwater spray on her lips, hear the pounding of the surf.

Her mind went over the details, ticking them off one by one. She'd contact an attorney and leave instructions about the business. Not that she wanted any of the money. She wanted to forget Spirno Charter ever existed. Maybe she could ask Mary to mind the phones and she could leave right away. Maybe . . .

With a flash of clarity, she saw what she was doing. Running away again. "No!" she said aloud. "Damnit, no. I've run as far as I'm going to."

She had come here to take a stand against her family and be in control of her life. Leaving at the first sign of trouble would only prove she hadn't learned a thing. This was her business—well, half of it, anyway—and no one, not even Mac, could take that away from her.

Anger joined her other emotions, burning hotter and brighter than the sun. He'd tried to take away her choice! Of all the pigheaded, insensitive . . .

And what about their relationship? Did he plan to dispose of that as neatly? She wouldn't let him dismiss what had happened between them as though it meant nothing. She loved him. For the first time in her life, she loved a man. And she was willing to fight for that love. But she wouldn't let him call all the shots. Not anymore.

From where she stood, there were two explanations for his behavior. First, he really didn't want her around. The thought that he resented her was like a fist crushing her heart, but she forced herself to examine the evidence. He'd been resistant when she arrived. But since then, things had gone surprisingly well. And in the last week, he'd seemed very happy to have her in his bed.

The second explanation was that he was still convinced she would be better off without him. That he was unable to be responsible enough, whatever that meant. If that were true, she was going to have to convince him that they belonged together—but only if he agreed they were equals. She couldn't stay with Mac if he insisted on running her life.

Turning away from the window, she sank into her chair and rested her head in her hands. The muscles in her back and neck clenched uncomfortably. How was she supposed to make Mac listen to her when he didn't want to? She'd have to confront him about the loan to buy her out and . . . She looked at the calendar.

In three days, she was supposed to meet Mac in the Keys and sail the *Amata* back to the marina. Over twenty-four hours alone at sea: no phones, no interruptions, no place for him to get off the boat. Trapped in confined quarters, he'd have no choice except to listen.

Mac stared out at the ocean and wished he were anywhere but there. Executive retreats were easy duty and in the past he'd always enjoyed them. The cook and maid came from an agency. All he had to do was find a good fishing area, drop anchor, and sit in the sun for three days.

This trip, however, he had too much time to think. He spent his days listening for the sound of Amy's voice and his nights lying awake wishing for her warm, willing body next to his. And every moment in between, he wrestled with his guilt. He should have told her about the loan.

It had been one thing when he'd applied to the bank. Based on his own calculations, he'd had only a slim chance of getting the funds. For the past few weeks he'd begun wishing he would be turned down for the money. At least then the responsibility for having Amy stay would have been taken out of his hands. But knowing a loan officer as a friend had turned out to be both good and bad news. With the combination of an increased business line of credit and a mortgage on the house, he'd get the amount he needed. But now he had to let her go.

What was he going to say? he wondered. Would she understand he was doing it for her? She deserved more than he could offer. She deserved a man who would guarantee he'd always put her first and do the right thing. A man who knew the rules and abided by them.

He'd tell her after they sailed back to the office. They'd have a last few hours together, then he'd explain why he had to buy her out. For the first time in his life, he was doing what he should, rather than what he wanted. Funny how badly that made him feel.

Amy unloaded the supplies from the car and carried them to the boat. After stowing her gear, she set to work. The food was put away in the cupboards, with the perishables tucked into the tiny refrigerator. This was it, she thought as she stared at the tiny cabin. She'd have it out with Mac and one way or the other, they'd get the issue of the partnerships settled . . . both the professional and the personal.

Climbing back to the cockpit, she started the diesel engine, then turned on and checked the radio. The gauges were all normal, the diesel tank was full. She shut off the motor. Anger and apprehension battled it out in her stomach. Currently anger was winning, but the fight wasn't over yet.

Standing on the roof of the cabin, Amy unsnapped the blue weather cloth covering the mainsail, then checked to see if it had been folded correctly. The lines were hanging straight and free of tangles. Then she stepped back into the cockpit to have the marine operator connect her to the office.

She had barely finished telling Mary that they would be leaving soon, when she heard a familiar voice from the slip.

"Permission to come aboard, captain," Mac said.

She drew in a deep breath for courage and turned to face him. "Permission granted."

Her eyes took in the strong lines of his face, studying the the firm jaw, the smiling lips, then returning to meet his gaze. Would she be able to keep her anger in check until they were at sea? Could he read the truth in her expression?

But he didn't give her any more opportunity to wonder. With a long stride, he crossed the cockpit and moved to gather her in his arms.

"I've missed you," he said.

"Me, too." Her voice was all-business as she side-stepped his embrace. "Let's get underway. Then we can, ah, talk."

"Okay." His dark eyes filled with confusion, but he made no further attempt to touch her.

She hesitated by the helm, almost willing to give in and let him take her to the place that needed no words, but this was too important. *She* was too important.

Heat coiled in her belly, but it wasn't desire or fear or even indecision. It was plain old, unladylike rage. For three days she'd simmered and now she was ready to let loose. Keep it calm, she told herself. Calm but honest.

Mac opened the hatch to the rear cabin and tossed his gear down on the floor, next to hers. For a second, she allowed her gaze to linger on the wide bed. Would they be sharing it tonight?

She forced her lips into a smile. "I've already done the check and called into the office."

Mac grinned. "You're the captain."

"So, I am." Straightening her shoulders, she started the engine. "Prepare to cast off."

He jumped on the dock and untied the lines. At her signal, he tossed them onto the bow and returned to the boat.

Easing them slowly into reverse, Amy backed the long, slender craft out of its slip. She kept the sails down until they'd cleared the marina and were close to the open ocean. While Mac raised the mainsail, she loosened the roller furling and let out the jib. The sails hung limply for a second, then snapped once or twice and caught the breeze. She cut the engine and let the wind move them forward.

The course back to their dock was fairly straightforward. For the next hour there was only the sound of the sea, broken by the occasional instruction.

She checked the chart, then glanced around. They were several miles from land. As far as the eye could see was water. It was time to stand up for herself or lose her self-respect forever.

She looked over at him. Mac sat with his back to the cabin, his long tanned legs stretched out on the cushion. A baseball cap was pulled down over his eyes as he read his boating magazine.

Her heart stumbled, then resumed its rapid beating in her chest.

"I know about the loan."

For a moment there was no response and she wondered if she'd simply thought the statement. Then the magazine slipped from his hands and he swung his feet to the deck.

"Who told you?"

The tone of his voice gave nothing away, but his question stole her last hope that there had been a mistake. "That's not important, is it? The point is, I know."

Mac took off the hat and ran his fingers through his black hair. Replacing the cap, he adjusted the brim and stared at the ground. "Amy, I guess you're upset, but—"

"Upset?" she repeated with a loud, angry tone. "You bet! What were you thinking of? How dare you go behind my back and get a loan to buy me out? It was underhanded and dishonest and just plain mean. Why didn't you talk to me about what you were feeling? If you hate having me around that much, you should have said something. You betrayed me. Is everything between us a lie?''

''No, of course not.'' He raised his eyes to meet hers. Torment and pain mingled in his face. ''I never meant to hurt you with this. I'm doing what's best for both of us.''

''No. You're doing what's easiest for you.''

''Amy, I—''

She cut him off with a glare. ''What you did was make the decision for me. I'm not a child. You had no right.''

''I thought . . .'' He held out one hand as if to offer her an explanation tied up in a neat package. ''I did it all for *you*. I know it was wrong to make the decision without consulting you, but my intentions were the best.''

''We're partners. Why won't you accept that?''

''I do. You've been practically running the whole business for the last month.''

''And the first chance you have, you try and get a loan to buy me out. Not very sporting of you.''

He rested his forearms on his thighs and linked his hands together. ''You're talking as though I hate sharing the business with you. I don't. In fact, I like having you around.''

She could feel her anger starting to fade. ''You sure don't act like it.''

Their eyes met. ''I'd never hurt you on purpose.''

She searched his face for the truth. ''But do you trust me?''

''Absolutely.'' His answer was instant and sincere.

''Then why are you trying to get rid of me?''

He turned to look out at the ocean. ''You're the most

important part of my life. I feel responsible for you. If you were gone, I wouldn't have to worry about being bad for you." He shrugged. "I just wanted to help."

"Could you explain how having me sell you my half of the business is going to help me?"

He shifted uncomfortably on the cushion. "You'd get another job and meet people. I know we have this thing between us, but seriously, Amy, you've got to admit, I'm the wrong guy for you. Just because I love you doesn't make it right."

"Geez, you're as bad as my mother. There you go again, taking my freedom away. *I* decide what's right and wrong for me. No one else."

She stood up to pace, then realized there was nowhere to pace to. The cockpit wasn't even six-feet wide. Great. And having the confrontation on the boat had been *her* idea. She was so angry, she wanted to throw something. She glanced at Mac. Maybe she could toss him overboard and see how he felt about swimming the rest of the way.

Oh, the nerve of that man, telling her he was getting rid of her so that she could find someone else. As if saying he loved her would make everything all right.

Love? She paused in mid-fume and spun to face him. "Love? Did you say you love me?"

He nodded, looking as miserable as a wet cat.

A string of curses that would have made Freddy sit up and take notice filled the air. "Are all men this pigheaded or are you the exception?" She raised her hand to halt his answer. "Never mind. I don't want to know. Do you mean to tell me you were going to let me walk out of your life, even though you love me?"

"Yes. I'm not responsible or any of those things you

need." He stood up and faced her. "I'm just a man, Amy. I've tried to stay out of your life and look what's happened. I don't want to interfere, but I can't promise I'll ever change. I don't come with any guarantees for happiness. I'm self-centered, opinionated, and impatient. Don't sell yourself short. You could have anyone."

If she'd ever thought of doubting his love for her, his willingness to sacrifice his own happiness for hers made the message as bright and vivid as the sun. He stood before her, warning her away, not knowing his words would keep her with him always.

He loved her! She had to make him see reason.

"Mac, there are no guarantees, ever. When you were growing up, you did a lot of things your father didn't approve of. But you're not that kid anymore. You're a responsible adult. Look at all you've done with the business. And me. When I showed up I was scared, but you gave me a chance to find out what I was capable of."

He looked skeptical. "I didn't want to share the business with you."

"But you did."

He shrugged. "I didn't have a whole hell of a lot of choice."

"Sure. But you could have been mean or difficult."

"I would have bought you out if I'd had the money."

"True." She smiled. "I think keel-hauling is a suitable punishment." Touching his forearm, she moved closer. "I'm not looking for perfect. I want a partner."

The corner of his mouth twisted down. "Some partner. I seduced you."

She paused and smiled slowly. "No. As I recall, I seduced you."

It was like pouring kerosene on an open fire. The explosion wiped away all her emotions except desire.

"You think so," he said, stepping closer.

"Absolutely." Her hands drifted up his chest and over his shoulders. "I believe it began with something like this."

Drawing his head down closer, she traced the shape of his mouth with her tongue. His low moan of pleasure drifted over her skin like a caress. She fumbled slightly, then found the helm lock and clicked it into place.

"Very responsible," he murmured as he picked her up in his arms. "How long do we have?"

"I don't have to change course for at least two hours."

He shook his head in dismay. "Not nearly long enough, but I suppose I could work fast."

"No," she said, as he stepped into the aft cabin and placed her on the bed. "I'll change it when the time comes. I wouldn't want to break your rhythm."

"Speaking of rhythm . . ." His fingers searched for and found the puckered nipple straining against her top. "There's a lot to be said for working against the current."

She arched her back. "I'd like a demonstration."

They surfaced for a short time to change the course and then a few hours later to grab some food. They napped and loved and talked, and it was close to midnight before Amy pushed back the hatch and really noticed the weather.

Instead of bright stars, the sky was filled with heavy

blackness. The wind was stronger and the waves higher. A sudden gust jerked the boat to starboard, while water broke over the bow.

"We've got a problem," she called back to Mac. "There's a storm."

He pulled on his clothing. "What did the weather report say?"

"There was a squall forming to the southwest, but it was supposed to blow itself out."

"Maybe it changed its mind. You get dressed and I'll check the radio."

She tugged on shorts and a T-shirt, slipped into her deck shoes, then pulled foul weather gear out of a compartment below the bed.

"Any news?" she asked when she climbed onto the deck and handed him his jacket.

"Yeah. It's heading right for us." He had to shout to be heard above the rapidly rising wind. Emergency lights cast an eerie yellow glow on the cockpit and into the darkness beyond. "We've got to get the sails down." He buttoned up the protective gear.

She nodded, then began cranking the roller furling to retract the jib. Mac moved to the side and loosened the line on the boom. The length of aluminum whipped back and forth until he captured it against his chest. Working quickly, he pulled the sail down and tied it in place.

Amy found and snapped on her lifeline, then turned to Mac. A pocket of wind hit the craft, swinging the loose boom toward him. She cried out and lunged forward, but she was too late. It cracked against his back, sending him sprawling. He fell half across the bench, his head hitting the deck, his left forearm slamming into the steel winch.

"Mac!" She dropped to his side. "Mac! Are you all right?"

There was no response. She turned him over and touched his face. His eyes were closed, his skin gray in the yellow light.

"Mac, no. Don't do this to me. You have to be okay. I need you. I love you. I can't lose you now."

Stinging rain fell from the heavens. Above her, the boom continued to sway with the motion of the boat. Working quickly, she tied it in place, then crouched down beside Mac. Before she could decide what to do, he groaned.

"W—what happened?" He opened his eyes. As he went to move his arm, he swore. "Amy?"

"How do you feel?"

He winced. "Like hell. I think my arm is broken."

"Oh, God." Stay calm, she told herself, trying to remember what she'd learned in her nautical first-aid class. Her priority was to get Mac secure and stabilized. "Can you move to the deck?" She pointed to the protected corner next to the main cabin.

"I think so." He slid his legs down, then lowered himself to the deck, groaning as he cradled his arm close to his chest. She snapped the lifeline onto his jacket. There was a rapidly swelling bump on his forehead, but no sign of blood.

She went quickly into the main cabin and grabbed anything she could think of that might help. The rain poured in through the hatch and pooled on the carpet. On her trip out, she pulled the cover shut behind her.

"Here." She handed him a nylon-coated blanket,

then dropped to her knees and opened the first aid kit. There were piles of bandages and ointments, creams and painkillers, but nothing for a break. "I was afraid of that," she muttered, brushing the rain out of her eyes. "Okay, I'm going to have to immobilize your arm." She pulled out the long wooden spoon she'd stuck in the waistband of her shorts. "I'll try not to hurt you."

"I'd appreciate that." His dark eyes were clouded with pain, but she saw the brave smile clinging to his lips.

The wind whistled around, threatening to rip the wood from her hands. She rested the spoon under his forearm, then wrapped gauze around him to hold it in place. He jerked once, then was still.

She rocked onto her heels and looked at him. "Do you want a painkiller?"

"No. I'm fine. You'd better get this boat on course or we'll never make it back."

"Shouldn't I call the Coast Guard?"

"No. With the storm coming up this suddenly, they've probably got some life or death emergencies. I trust you, Amy."

He sounded confident. If only she felt the same. "Okay. If you're sure." She took a box of juice out of her coat pocket and handed it to him. "Wish me luck."

When she checked their heading, she was relieved that the storm seemed to be blowing them slightly toward the shore. With luck, they weren't too far off course. The engine started on the first try and she breathed a quick prayer of thanks. Maybe they'd make it after all.

The wheel was stiff in her hand, as if the rudder

resisted. She jerked it to port with all her might and slowly the boat turned toward home.

She wasn't sure how long the wind and rain lasted. Beyond the emergency light, the world was a black void of rain and turbulent sea. The salty spray stung her eyes and cracked her lips.

Through the night, her fingers ached, then grew numb. Every half hour or so, she crouched down to check on Mac, but he always assured her he was fine. It was impossible to tell if he had a concussion, but he stayed awake and coherent. They had a makeshift meal of fruit and water, then she resumed her place at the helm.

She'd never felt such fear before. It was just the two of them in a tiny craft against the might of the ocean. In her heart, she knew their fate rested in her inexperienced hands. For long stretches of time, she was calm. Then the panic would build up and threaten to choke her. Her legs trembled from keeping her steady while the deck bucked and rolled like a champion bronco. Even her ears ached from the pounding of the waves and the roaring of the storm. When it seemed easier to give in to the forces rallying against them, she made herself remain at the helm, holding them on course. She'd get Mac to safety, or die trying.

The rain let up slowly. At first she thought it was her imagination, but then she saw the shape of a cloud, then another. The sky grew light. A seagull drifted past the bow. Even the sea became smooth and flat to meet the coming dawn.

"M–Mac?" She pointed to the horizon and the long stretch of land that was home. "We made it."

He smiled, the curve of his lips drooping with weariness. "I never doubted you for a minute, princess. You're a hell of a woman. When we get back to dry land, I'm going to lock us in the bedroom and not come out for a week."

She knelt beside him and touched his face. "How do you feel?"

"Like a new man." Dark eyes met and held her own. She couldn't read the emotions flashing there, but her heart fluttered for a moment. He turned his head and kissed her palm, then glanced back at her. "I may not be the best man for you, and I can't promise I won't interfere again, but I'll be damned if I'll let you go. I love you. Amy Morgan, will you marry me?"

"Ahoy! Is this the *Amata*?"

The loudspeaker belonged to a Coast Guard cutter. Amy sprang to her feet and began to wave. "Yes! I have an injured crew member."

"Your office contacted us and said you were caught in the storm. Slow your boat. We'll come alongside."

Within a matter of moments, two men had boarded the boat. They helped Mac to his feet and took him onto the cruiser. An officer leaned over the side.

"You're about a mile or so from shore. Do you want a tow?"

Amy grinned. "No, thank you. I'll take her back myself." She waved at Mac. "I'll see you soon, sailor."

The powerful craft drifted away, then the engines roared into life. She raised the mainsail and began the last leg of the journey home.

ELEVEN

"All right, Mr. Spirno. Any time you're ready."

The nurse handed him the fresh set of clothing, then left the room. Mac wondered who'd brought them, but didn't want to call her back to ask. What if it wasn't Amy?

From the dock, he'd been transported to the hospital. They'd set his arm, then decided to keep him overnight for observation. The bump on his head was painful, but not life threatening.

Yesterday afternoon he'd had a parade of visitors. Everyone from the office, his father, even Lynn had stopped by. But there'd been no Amy. Last night, right before visiting hours had ended, she'd breezed in, offered a quick hello and a kiss, then left. There'd been no explanation as to where she'd been all day. He knew she hadn't slept all night during the storm, but still. She could have at least responded to his proposal.

As Mac buttoned up his shirt, he cursed softly. Had

he waited too long to declare himself? Was she still upset that he had wanted to buy her out? Didn't she know everything he'd done was simply an expression of his love and concern? And that he'd learned his lesson about trying to run her life?

The door swung open. "Yo! Bossman!" Bob strolled into the room and grinned. "You're looking fine this morning. No one would guess you almost bought the farm out there." He held out his hand. "It's good to see you, buddy."

Mac smiled, hoping his disappointment didn't show. After all that had happened between them, he'd been expecting Amy to pick him up. Was this her way of saying she didn't want to marry him?

Before he could convince himself one way or the other, they'd left the hospital and were heading toward the ocean. He glanced at his employee. "This isn't the way to the house."

"I know." Bob refused to look at him. "I, ah, thought you might want to go to the office. You know, kinda check things out."

"Not really," Mac said, leaning back in the seat and cradling his arm. He'd rather avoid being humiliated in front of a crowd. If Amy was going to reject him, better that it should happen in the privacy of their home. "I'm still tired."

"Yeah, ah, okay. Just let me pick something up, then I'll take you right to the house."

Bob sounded unusually tense, but Mac was too concerned about other things to press him for an explanation. Was Amy giving him the brush-off?

They drove into the parking lot. Bob stepped out of the car and looked back at him expectantly.

"I'll just wait here," Mac said.

"But, boss." Bob swallowed uncomfortably. "You have to . . . I mean, there's something you should see."

"What are you talking about?"

"I . . . There's . . . Listen, dude, just come with me for a minute, okay?"

Bob's harsh voice was so out of character that Mac didn't think of doing anything but obey. He got out of the car and followed the younger man down the ramp.

The air was warm, the sky clear. There was no hint of the storm that had almost claimed his and Amy's life. His trained eye took in the slips, noting which boats were tied up and which were out on charters.

Something bobbing at the end of the dock caught his attention and he moved closer. It was Freddy's old yawl. The wood gleamed in the light of day. The stern bumped against the planking of the slip and he caught a glimpse of what looked like a new name.

His heart sank. Someone had bought the boat. He sighed. In the back of his mind had been the fantasy that Freddy would save it for him. All and all, he'd spent the last week or so really making a mess of his life. He ought to . . .

A woman stepped out of the cabin. For a moment, Mac thought he really had died in the storm and this was his reward. Amy turned toward him and smiled. Her hair shone like gold in the morning light. The love shining in her eyes threatened to blind him. Moving with liquid grace, she stepped onto the dock and pointed to the boat.

"What do you think?"

He stopped a foot away from her. "You bought it?"

She nodded. "Check out the new name."

He leaned over and started to laugh. In big bold letters, the stern of the ship proclaimed: *First Mate*. "That's telling the world." His smile faded. "But who does it refer to?"

"Me. Yesterday, I never got a chance to accept the proposal." She shifted slightly and looked up at him. "This boat is your wedding present. If you still want me."

"Want you? Oh, Amy, don't you know you're all I've ever wanted?"

Suddenly, she was in his arms and they were sealing the arrangement with long, slow kisses that threatened his weakened condition.

She pulled back and looked up at him. "You aren't still thinking of trying to buy me out, are you?"

"Never."

"Good. Because when I make up my mind, there's no going back. I love you, Napoleon Christopher Spirno, and this is one partnership you'll never get out of."

SHARE THE FUN . . .
SHARE YOUR NEW-FOUND TREASURE!!

You don't want to let your new books out of your sight?
That's okay. Your friends can get their own. Order below.

No. 62 FOR SERVICES RENDERED by Ann Patrick
Nick's life is in perfect order until he meets Claire!

No. 63 WHERE THERE'S A WILL by Leanne Banks
Chelsea goes toe-to-toe with her new, unhappy business partner.

No. 64 YESTERDAY'S FANTASY by Pamela Macaluso
Melissa always had a crush on Morgan. Maybe dreams do come true!

No. 65 TO CATCH A LORELEI by Phyllis Houseman
Lorelei sets a trap for Daniel but gets caught in it herself.

No. 66 BACK OF BEYOND by Shirley Faye
Dani and Jesse are forced to face their true feelings for each other.

No. 67 CRYSTAL CLEAR by Cay David
Max could be the end of all Crystal's dreams . . . or just the beginning!

No. 68 PROMISE OF PARADISE by Karen Lawton Barrett
Gabriel is surprised to find that Eden's beauty is not just skin deep.

No. 69 OCEAN OF DREAMS by Patricia Hagan
Is Jenny just another shipboard romance to Officer Kirk Moen?

Meteor Publishing Corporation
Dept. 592, P. O. Box 41820, Philadelphia, PA 19101-9828

Please send the books I've indicated below. Check or money order (U.S. Dollars only)—no cash, stamps or C.O.D.s (PA residents, add 6% sales tax). I am enclosing $2.95 plus 75¢ handling fee for *each* book ordered.

Total Amount Enclosed: $_____.

____ No. 91	____ No. 52	____ No. 58	____ No. 64
____ No. 47	____ No. 53	____ No. 59	____ No. 65
____ No. 48	____ No. 54	____ No. 60	____ No. 66
____ No. 49	____ No. 55	____ No. 61	____ No. 67
____ No. 50	____ No. 56	____ No. 62	____ No. 68
____ No. 51	____ No. 57	____ No. 63	____ No. 69

Please Print:
Name _____

Address _____ Apt. No. _____

City/State _____ Zip _____

Allow four to six weeks for delivery. Quantities limited.